MUSINGS FROM
THE MAGIC DESK

Leslie Medalie

Musings from the Magic Desk ©
Published by Leary & Company Publishing

Copyright © 2025 by Leslie Medalie

ISBN: 979-8-218-73066-6
ISBN 979-8-218-74854-8 (e-book)

First printing 2025

Cover (background) photograph, "Enchanting Shores"
by Steven Koppel, owner of Expressions Gallery

Printed and bound in the United States of America.

1 3 5 7 9 8 6 4 2

www.MusingsfromtheMagicDesk.com

ACKNOWLEDGMENTS

Writing *Musings from the Magic Desk* provided me great comfort during a challenging time. As my family grappled with a stream of hardships, my recently inherited heirloom desk seemed to offer its own mysterious answers, helping me find strength and guidance. Within its secret compartments, I discovered the novena to Saint Martha and other special signs that aided in creating the novel.

I thank my wonderful and supportive husband, Seth, for his constant encouragement; my children, Ryan and Caitlin, for their perennial love; my exceptional coach and editor, Joanne Moyle, who expertly guided me through this process; and Steven Koppel, owner of Expressions Gallery, for allowing us to use his breathtaking photo of *Enchanting Shores* on the cover.

I hope that this story provides inspiration to all its readers.

CHAPTER 1
Clouds

It was the most beautiful late summer day in the English countryside. The sky sparkled like a sapphire, with clouds swaying in the breeze, creating gentle waves in the fescue grass. It was mesmerizing—as breathtaking as one might imagine heaven to be. It was so tranquil, a far cry from the battlefield of Crimea, where English soldiers were fighting a war they did not fully comprehend while dying by the thousands.

Martha took in the picturesque scene around her as she strolled the meadows, seeking shade from a sturdy, century-old maple tree. It was Tuesday, and she was here in England on a mission. Having just arrived and becoming acclimated to the scenes around her, Martha appeared as a woman in her prime. Her presence seemed iridescent. Wearing a diaphanous white dress and waist-length auburn hair with fiery red highlights pulled back with a silver ribbon, her piercing emerald eyes sparkled against her porcelain complexion.

Martha took great pride in her work and was exceptionally skilled at her trade. Her assignment was a complicated one, and she was unsure if she could accomplish exactly what was asked of her. Martha's work was always done on Tuesdays—rain, shine, sleet, snow—in turmoil or strife. She was consistently surprised that so many asked for her by name, and she was equally amazed by the dedication of those who requested her services.

Martha was raised as a humble house woman who served and cared for others. Her home had been almost as busy as a bustling inn, with Martha and her siblings entertaining the great minds of the day who passed through their village. However, she felt an ever-present sense of anxiousness in the company of many, and her mentors chided her for caring more for her cooking and cleaning than taking the time to absorb her guests' illuminating discussions.

But Martha had an open mind and took the enlightening lessons from her visitors to heart. As time went on, she would better understand her unique place—her special mission—to become the protector of so many who prayed for her assistance in the most difficult of situations.

"Saint Martha, I resort to your protection and faith. I offer this candle which I shall burn every Tuesday," the novena would begin. Believers had been calling on her for centuries, and she answered each one that she could, perhaps not with the exact outcome that they sought, but with a revelation for each that could give them the strength they needed.

Over the years, Martha had answered many prayers—from a mother pleading for healing for her sick child to a lost soul seeking forgiveness and guidance—to a grandfather begging for mercy for his imprisoned adult son. Each mission was chosen based on the seeker's belief in the novena and their inner understanding that, though Martha may provide a reprieve, their specific request might not be granted exactly as requested. Martha's purpose was to provide hope, courage, and resilience for those who prayed the novena. She was always up to the task and took great pride in her work and the comfort it provided.

Today, her mission was to assist a young soldier's wife. Clara was only eighteen years old, and her handsome soldier husband, Arthur, had been sent to Crimea where the Crown had recently deployed him—along with thousands of others to fight in the war. Clara had heard about the dire situation of those on the battlefield, and she understood that many of the young lads sent to fight on behalf of the Queen and her allied countries were dying every day. They would fall not only on the battlefield but also to disease in equal numbers.

It was the seventh Tuesday of the novena, and Clara diligently prayed, begging Martha for her divine intervention on behalf of Arthur. There were few Catholics in England in the mid-1800s, but each Tuesday, Clara would venture to the church closest to her home, light a candle, and beseech Martha to keep Arthur alive so that he could return to her. Legend had it that Martha possessed the strength to slay dragons and that her powers would "grant everything, no matter how difficult, before the eighth Tuesday" for those who observed the novena ritual.

"Dear Saint Martha, hear my plea," Clara prayed. "This war is unbearable, and it may ultimately leave our country without a generation of men; please help Arthur return to me. He is all I have." Just a year earlier, at seventeen years old, Clara had lost her father in a work accident and then her mother to despair. With no siblings to lean on, she prayed fervently for the future of her life with Arthur.

Clara was a beautiful young woman with a petite frame, topaz blue eyes, and long, wavy blonde hair. She looked just as her mother had, and inherited her deep sense of loyalty, and fierce love of family as well. Clara's childhood had been a happy one. The family resided in a small single-family dwelling in the English countryside in a village that had the right of entry to the British rail system, so Clara's father had easy access to the larger city of Manchester for work.

Clara's father traveled daily to his work as a black-smith, an important role in early Victorian England that would gradually diminish in significance as industrialization swept the country. When Clara was young, black-smiths were regarded as a respected profession requiring a unique combination of skill and courage to withstand the two-thousand-degree inferno of the molten fire forge that heated the metal until it was soft enough to work with. Clara's father took pride in his expertise, but over the years, his health suffered from the toils of his labor. With his sleeves rolled up, his hands and arms were often charred by the fire. The tools were blazing hot; just the slightest erroneous move could result in horrendous burns.

Since the family was Catholic, rather than members of the Church of England, they worshipped a few townships away, making their day-to-day socialization quieter, particularly for Clara who was an only child. Schooled at home by her mother, with a focus on domestic skills and occasional music training from local teachers, Clara was a content and creative child with a vivid imagination. Although her family only left the town for work or worship, she often daydreamed about the exotic lands she heard people discussing after Sunday Mass. England had other territories where any Englishman was free to explore, including the islands and colonies of British North America—which were the latest adventure for many inquisitive sailors. Clara soaked up all the chatter and envisioned these exciting new locales.

When Clara's father suddenly passed away after a tragic accident at the shop, her mother was so heartbroken that she took to her bed, neither eating nor drinking, until she, too, joined him in death several months later. Clara understood that her mother could not live without her father, and thankfully, she had Arthur by her side to support her during this devastating time.

Arthur had courted Clara since her sixteenth birthday, when he saw her walking through the town. A handsome young man with golden-streaked hair and pale blue eyes, Arthur was tall with a sinewy build. His father was the town's most well-known woodworker, and Arthur was apprenticing with him. Following her parents' untimely deaths, their young courtship quickly led to an engagement and wedding when Clara turned eighteen. The marriage took place in the Anglican church, but Clara and Arthur received a secret blessing from her Catholic priest so she could honor her parents' traditions.

After her parents' deaths, Clara's grief was overwhelming. Without Arthur's love and support, she was unsure she would have made it through. The two moved into her parents' small home and slowly healed from the sorrow. Arthur ventured out from his apprenticeship with his father, finding work in a local wood craftsman's shop where he made musical instruments from locally felled trees. The shop also made fine furniture chiseled from the trunks of trees from the lush nearby forest.

At this point in their young lives, the two worked tirelessly in order to afford to keep Clara's childhood home. The heaviness of grief slowly faded, and the inner peace brought on by their young love began to return to Clara. However, their newfound contentment would not endure. Just as Arthur and Clara were starting to settle into their new lives together, Arthur was called up for military duty to fight in Crimea.

The war had left Clara alone and frightened for their future, but thankfully, she had her work to keep her occupied. A gifted seamstress, Clara had learned how to sew as a child, just like her mother. Her family was not poor but certainly not wealthy, so it was important for the women to be able to make a penny to add to the family coffers. Sewing was something that brought both mother and daughter satisfaction and a sense of worthy accomplishment.

"Take in the beauty around you, dear child," Clara's mother would say as they sat side by side with needle in hand. "With simple fabric and thread, you can bring your visions to life. Learn by observing and practicing, and your skills will serve you well."

"But, Mother," Clara would respond. "Someday I want to buy my own fine dresses in one of the village shops, instead of having to sew them myself."

"Humility is God's greatest gift to us. Always remember that, and you will be provided for," her mother would retort.

Clara became a skillful designer and creator of lovely, fashionable dresses for the ladies of society. Now, more than ever, her work as a seamstress was essential to augment Arthur's soldier's wages, enabling them to remain in her parents' former home, where her sewing studio was now located. With Arthur in Crimea, Clara led a life of solitude, except for the small talk with the ladies requiring her sewing services. She kept busy all week with her labors but spent her free time in prayer. She was often seen making the long walk to her church, followed by lengthy strolls in the meadows and forest.

But today was different from recent days. When she awoke, she immediately sensed it. The weather was so crisp and inviting that, after going to church to say her novena, Clara strolled to the meadow at the edge of town. The fescue looked like the ocean on this day, the wind creating undulating ripples in the long grass. It was so verdant, and the distant trees seemed so robust and full. If Clara squinted, it seemed she could almost see a faint ethereal aura around those maple trees. This was a special day indeed, and she had a special favor to ask of Saint Martha, God, and the universe. The day just seemed ripe for a miracle.

Martha was also in the meadow that day, having found a comfortable spot beneath the largest of all the maple trees to contemplate her work. She reflected on Clara and her prayerful intentions while beginning to formulate a plan to assist. The novena had been recited seven times, with next Tuesday marking the eighth—the final day of the novena when a resolution was required. But how was she to save a soldier in Crimea this week, knowing that his continued tour of duty the following week could bring death? Martha understood that the only way she could respond to Clara's pleas was to protect Arthur as best she could. She considered how she would accomplish this seemingly impossible mission; but, of course, that was precisely her calling.

Martha daydreamed as she watched the clouds engage in their usual pageantry, undulating in the sky above her. "You see, if you observe the clouds on just the right day, you might uncover the answers you seek. It requires imagination and a belief in miracles, but the clues are there," one of Martha's guests had explained when he visited her home centuries ago.

On this day, two clouds appeared to be engaged in a vigorous battle—one forcefully charging forth with a magnitude of tremendous strength, while the other resembled a lone soldier steadfastly holding his ground. The formation of larger clouds unleashed a bombardment on the soldier; the aggressors loomed large and ominous in comparison to the lone fighter confronting them from his position. Yet, the soldier remained resolute, and instead of retreating from the projectiles being hurled, he opened his arms and welcomed them. Just then, the wind changed; the clouds collided and then parted. The only silhouette left in the sky was that of the foot soldier, weaponless, now seemingly advancing toward yet another large cloud formation, which appeared to be a welcoming battalion of diverse troops.

The answer was truly in the clouds. Arthur must prove himself within the ranks and be recognized for his valor. And the only way for that to become a reality was through his bravery and cunning. There was no time to spare. Martha needed to formulate a plan for Arthur and act immediately upon it to change the course of events and eventually return him to Clara.

Clara did not notice the large maple tree at the far end of the field; she was too engrossed in walking through the meadow, taking in the beauty surrounding her. As she connected with the earth's life force, thoughts of Arthur in battle flooded her mind—the horrors of war and the little he wrote of them to keep her calm at home. Today marked the seventh Tuesday she had recited the novena to Saint Martha, and by next Tuesday, she hoped Arthur would be safe. Clara believed with all her heart and soul in Saint Martha and her extraordinary powers, feeling a sense of peace on this day, knowing that her prayers might soon be answered.

As she continued walking, her eyes grew heavy. She realized she had become bone tired from the relentless pace of her work and the disquieting thoughts of her husband on the battlefield. The majestic maple tree was now in sight—it stood regally in the meadow, well over a century old. It looked inviting and comforting, drawing Clara closer. As she moved slowly forward, she thought of nothing but sitting under it to seek its comforting shade.

Not far from Clara, Martha lowered her gaze from the clouds and smiled. She loved how God and the universe always possessed the right plan if she was clever enough to seek it out and trust in it. *But who was that approaching her?* Martha recognized immediately; it was Clara.

Martha had allowed herself to be part of the human world for just a little too long. Now, she had nowhere to turn without Clara confronting her. Saints and angels can live among us on this earth, but this was not the time to meet Clara.

Martha knew exactly what to do; she closed her eyes and melded her earthly being into the maple, seamlessly becoming part of its sturdy trunk and branches. She could feel the heart of its ancient life force, and it could feel hers, as the two became one.

Clara approached the maple. Maybe if she lay in this shaded spot under its refreshing leaves, she would feel better, she thought. Oddly, the area she chose to lie in was warm, as if someone had just been sitting in that same spot . . . She looked about but saw no one, letting the thought fade away. She drifted into sleep, thinking of Arthur and his impending return to her.

"Hello, Clara. I am Martha," a voice stated from the tree.

Is this a dream? Yes, it must be . . .

"Thank you for your dedication to the novena. I have heard your weekly prayers, and I will work to keep Arthur safe as you have requested. The road will not be easy, and the path may not be straightforward, but Arthur *will* return.

"You must be brave and resilient—he will need you to help him as he recovers from the horrors of war. Battle leaves indelible scars, yet you can, and will, help heal them. You are a special woman, Clara; use your gifts to help Arthur—and others."

Clara was jolted out of her dreamlike state. Did Saint Martha just visit her? Was it a vision? She had not seen Martha; she only heard her soothing voice while she rested beneath the majestic maple tree. She rose from her spot under the tree and began her long journey home, her heart filled with hope.

Martha watched Clara stroll through the meadow toward the township. She thanked the maple for harboring her as she gently ascended from within the bole of the tree into her human form once more. But this time, she allowed her wings to expand from behind her back. Martha did not typically display her wings, retracting them when encountering earthbound beings, but it was almost time for her to travel to the battlefield—and in her haste, she allowed them to unfurl freely.

Divinely beautiful at this moment, she appeared as a pure angel with an irresistible effervescence. Martha wrapped her arms around the maple, once more expressing her gratitude. Then, it was time to depart. She stepped away from the tree, spread her wings, and began her flight to Crimea.

At that exact moment, across the meadow, Clara tripped over a stone and stumbled onto the soft, mossy ground. As she fell, Clara gazed up at the sky. In a fleeting instant, she beheld the unimaginable—her beloved Saint Martha in flight—and she realized she had just witnessed a miracle.

The Crimean War would go down in history for the horrific conditions endured by soldiers—and the British death rates reached hundreds per day, with troops succumbing to cholera, dysentery, and skin diseases, resulting in as many deaths as those suffered on the battlefield. The winter leading up to the end of the war was long and bitterly cold. A menacing storm struck the Crimean Peninsula, destroying the British Army's tents and sinking several ships carrying much-needed medical supplies, food, and clothing for the troops.

Many times throughout the war, soldiers lacked essential supplies like soap, towels, and basins, while their uniforms became infested with bugs, fleas, and lice. The situation was unbearable, and many men began to suffer from the psychological effects of their conditions as well as the physical trauma of the battlefield.

As a young combatant with no military training, once Arthur joined the army he was immediately sent to the front line. The war was fought on land and sea and had been raging for almost two years, but it was slowly winding down, culminating with the Russian forces' losses that diminished their willingness to sustain the aggression.

Although there were large, well-known battles, smaller, day-to-day combat was also endured. Foot soldiers in trenches defended territorial gains and thwarted enemy advances. Advanced technologies of the day were also used in battle on both the ground and the seas, and both sides learned new methods of war.

The summer heat brought its own tribulations, such as mosquitoes, trench foot, and more. However, the troops were in better spirits than throughout the previous winter months, and supplies were somewhat more plentiful. Arthur had landed in a platoon of exceptional soldiers who were young and strong, and more than ready for the rigor of battle.

Arthur readily learned how to shoot, wield a sword, and fight in the fog of war. He did not allow himself to consider the souls he had taken; in war, there was no time for emotion or guilt. He listened intently to his commanders and wholeheartedly threw himself into the attack—or defense, as the case may be.

Arthur was a keen observer and listener. Although a foot soldier, he had recently heard of the courage of a private in the Royal Navy who had saved his entire ship and crew through the heroic act of disposing of a live shell that had been shot onto the deck by the enemy. Snatching the shell in his bare hands, he had thrown it into the ocean, where it safely detonated. His sharp-witted and selfless action saved many lives, and news of this youthful hero spread swiftly through the British ground troops and naval infantry.

The Russians were now using a wide range of these new technologies and had amassed a significant arsenal of exploding shells. Originally used to sink enemy warships, they were now bringing them to the battles on land. The shells could create havoc for the soldiers, frightening the horses, creating massive explosions, and breaking down troop lines.

Martha quietly arrived in Crimea that Tuesday evening. She hid amongst the clouds until nightfall to remain unseen, surveying Arthur and his battalion's position. She observed the Russians' position and the locations of the allied French, English, Turkish, and Sardinian forces. She knew that this week, she would need to guide Arthur in distinguishing himself from others in the rank and file.

That night, Martha visited Arthur in his dreams. "Arthur, it is I, Saint Martha. Clara has sent me to help you eventually return from this war to her. Stay calm, be brave, and remember what you have heard. Act decisively. This is your destiny; accept and embrace it."

Arthur jumped awake from the dream. What had he just heard? And what did it mean?

The following day, he would understand Martha's message.

It was a remarkably sunny morning, and Arthur had been requested by a commanding officer to assist with some of the campaign furniture—portable, practical pieces designed specifically for officers' use in the field. These wooden items were a defining feature of the higher ranks' tent quarters, offering small elements of comfort.

As a woodworker, Arthur would often help make or repair the pine chairs, desks, and beds used by the brigade generals and officers. It was a welcome reprieve from being in the trenches with his fellow soldiers—as well as a chance to be in the presence of these well-respected army leaders.

As Arthur began to walk from the senior officers' camp to head back to the soldiers' quarters, he contemplated his dream about Saint Martha the night before. Still confused as to its significance, he shook his head, determining that most likely it was just his mind attempting to distract him from the miserable conditions that faced him and his fellow soldiers daily.

Suddenly, Arthur heard an unusual sound coming from the eastern sky. Unfortunately, it was almost impossible to glance up in that direction with the intense sunlight beaming down.

Then he heard a thud.

He was just outside of the commanding general's tent when it dropped. There, right before his feet, was a live shell, which must have been launched by the enemy from the east.

Arthur acted quickly—and decisively. The shell was live but had not yet been discharged. He could hear a soft ticking sound and realized that it must be on a timer.

There was no time to waste. Without thinking that he might be running straight into the enemy lines, Arthur took the shell in his shaking hands and ran toward the eastern woods. Mustering every ounce of strength and courage in his body, he hurled the shell into the forest and ran directly back to the officers' tents, shouting that there was an impending attack.

Calculated to take out the top commanders of the brigade prior to a full-scale attack, the shell's blast could be heard throughout the camp. In a flash, a wildfire ignited in the tree line, smoking out the enemy troops who were hiding in the woods. The next hours saw a bloody battle, but due to Arthur's actions, the battalion leadership was intact, and the troops were mercifully spared.

The Russians' surprise attack had been thwarted, and their men finally retreated through the scorched woods.

Martha sighed with relief. Arthur had heeded her words and saved his brigade from a stealth attack meant to destroy their leadership. He had been resolute, and fearless, proving himself to be a heroic soldier.

It would take months before the war ended, but news of Arthur's courageous actions came via a letter from his commanding officer to Clara. Arthur was promoted from rank and file and moved to permanently assist the officers with any required woodworking, carpentry tasks, and designs.

Although he could not come directly back to her, Clara knew that he was in a safer position than manning the trenches and that, somehow, he had survived an attack that could have severely crippled his entire unit.

After the war ended, Arthur triumphantly returned to their village and became known as a war hero to all. Once home with his beloved Clara, Arthur's status in the town escalated due to the distinction of being awarded Britain's highest military designation.

In honor of his bravery, Arthur was one of over one hundred Crimean War veterans to receive the Victoria Cross, the Queen's medal awarded to recognize exceptional valor regardless of military rank. Clara beamed proudly at her husband as the Queen bestowed the Cross upon Arthur and the other brave soldiers in an elegant ceremony.

Martha gazed down upon the two young newlyweds. By the eighth day of the novena, she had answered Clara's prayers and helped Arthur handle a dangerous situation. The young couple may have had to wait for their reconciliation, but Arthur was alive, and Martha had granted Clara's prayer to bring him home to her. Clara and Arthur could now create a life together.

Over time, Arthur established himself as a sought-after wood crafter known for his exquisite harps and other instruments. With a keen interest in expanding his shop's offerings, Arthur also began to seek out wood from special trees to create intricate desks and home furnishings.

Clara's skills also spread through word of mouth throughout the local towns. Ladies would come by train or buggy, bringing their fabrics for Clara to create the most beautiful gowns, skirts, and jackets. Clara was especially clever at using trims and embellishments to make each garment distinctive.

They had survived the war, the deaths of Clara's parents, and were finally delighting in their individual pursuits, as well as their love for each other. It was the happiest of times.

Martha smiled; her mission was complete. It was time for her to answer the next novena.

But in her haste to hide from Clara that day in the meadow, she did not realize that she had accomplished something equally important—she had left a bit of the essence of her spirit within the mighty maple tree.

And that maple tree's mystical qualities were about to be revealed.

CHAPTER 2
Wonder

Clara and Arthur, now happily reunited, were becoming settled in Clara's family home, and were developing their respective work specialties. The only element missing was a child. But since they were so young, they felt sure that Clara would become pregnant at any time. As the months passed, each pushed aside their disappointment and prayed for the following month's bounty.

Since returning from Crimea, Arthur had been different than before the war. As Saint Martha had predicted, battle had left scars on his soul. He was quieter and more introverted than before, content to be holed up in his workshop for many hours working on his craft. He did not join Clara on her weekly retreats to church, so he missed the exciting tales from congregants about the local sailors heading off—or returning from—exciting adventures in British North America.

"Arthur, please let me know what is going on. You are so closed and reserved, and I am deeply concerned," Clara pleaded as Arthur continued to withdraw. "I love you so much and want to be here for you."

Arthur would stare blankly at Clara and shrug his shoulders, barely saying a word in return. If he did respond, it was consistently in regard to finances. "Clara, my work is very important now, and we need to build our future together. I have not abandoned you; I simply need time alone to do my work," was always the practical answer.

Contented to remain solitary, and utterly consumed by his woodworking, Arthur's skills were becoming exceptional. He began with harps—finding the intricacies of creating the beautiful instrument a soothing distraction from his racing thoughts of the battlefield. A harp could take an entire year to create, so he immersed himself in the process after being commissioned by a local aristocrat. But as he worked on the instrument, in his limited spare time he also began studying the making of desks, which truly fascinated him.

His harp-making would bring Arthur valuable revenue, but his desk-making would be for his family— something to treasure for generations to come—and pass down to his children, if God blessed them with little ones. Arthur began mulling over how to move his growing woodworking venture into a bigger space, and soon, he and Clara realized that her parents' small home would not be large enough to hold her seamstress business along with his craftsman workshop.

The couple began searching for a larger home and workspace for their growing enterprises and were surprised and delighted to discover a local inn for sale in the township. The inn featured four guest bedrooms, along with separate quarters to meet their family's needs. However, the most appealing aspect of the inn was the detached barn, which had been converted into a workspace—with ample room for both his woodworking and her sewing studios. With their savings and the proceeds from her parents' home sale, Arthur and Clara purchased the inn and moved into their new home base—and a new way of life.

"I do believe we should name our new establishment Martha's Meadowside Inn," Clara suggested to Arthur.

"Why Martha? Perhaps we should select a family name that can be passed on through the generations," Arthur countered.

"Arthur, I just *know* it should be named Martha, and it sounds so lovely—Martha's Meadowside Inn," she replied with a knowing smile. She thought to herself that it would be aptly named in tribute to her special saint and the beautiful meadow where it was situated.

Arthur, not nearly as engaged in the naming process as Clara, nodded in simple agreement.

Martha's Meadowside Inn would prove to become a labor of love. Clara took on the role of innkeeper alongside her sewing work, making her days feel almost never-ending. Arthur spent most of his day in the barn, focused on the commissioned harp and delving into the research of desk-making. Gradually, through word of mouth and its previous reputation as an inn, Arthur and Clara's latest business venture began to attract travelers.

Running an inn was a new experience for both of them. Clara took on the lion's share of the workload, handling the cleaning and cooking herself while making the bedrooms bright and comfortable with her custom-made curtains, duvets, and upholstery. Cooking was a completely new skill for Clara to learn, but the inn guests were only promised a morning meal, so toast, eggs, and bacon were the daily fare. Clara began enjoying innkeeping more than her sewing business and took on an apprentice to assist her with the seamstress tasks so she could focus more on her guests.

Saint Martha often quietly observed the couple now that they were innkeepers. As time passed, Martha became concerned about Arthur. When he first came home from the war and was awarded the Victoria Cross, everything seemed promising. But as she understood, war can ruin a soldier and crush the soul. Watching so many die—and being forced to take lives in battle—is a horrible ordeal, even though Arthur did not ask for this terrible assignment, nor boast of any valor in serving.

But Arthur was becoming less and less part of the world. While he spent hours in his workshop, he was slowly declining, both physically and mentally. Martha was saddened that, although she had fulfilled Clara's prayer to bring Arthur home, the life the couple was now leading was not what either had envisioned.

For her part, Clara had been blessed with a hopeful spirit. She remembered Martha's words about helping Arthur upon his return from war and fully understood that his emotional scars ran deep. She believed wholeheartedly that her love could conquer his malaise, so she devised her own plan to help Arthur recover from his depression.

"I know I can bring Arthur back to me," Clara contemplated while journaling. "I just need to find a way to restore joy to his life." Understanding Arthur's many worries about income, she devised a plan.

Now that she was an innkeeper and not as busy all day in the sewing room, she had time to create additional revenue sources for the inn. One that was particularly interesting to her was serving dinner for a small fee. She had become quite proficient at making simple breakfasts, so she decided it was time to offer a home-cooked dinner each evening.

As supper was the most elaborate meal served each day, Clara learned how to make interesting courses, including soups made from a slowly simmered broth, garden vegetables, and succulent chicken meat from the previous evening's roast.

She asked her fellow churchgoers each week for their favorite recipes and soon served fresh pork loin from the town butcher with sage and onion stuffing alongside roasted root vegetables. Some evenings, she selected local pheasant, which she cooked slowly all afternoon with fresh thyme and rosemary from the garden.

If the fishmonger had secured a good catch, she would choose salmon or cod for the evening meal. Clara would pan-fry the pieces, experimenting with various flavorings, such as onions or capers, and then set them atop her delicious mashed potatoes, finishing the meal with a dessert course of bread pudding. The inn guests were delighted with Clara's growing culinary skills, and Clara was equally proud of her most recent accomplishment.

Over time, the dinner service at Martha's Meadowside Inn became so popular that others in the village inquired if they might be able to enjoy an inn meal from time to time. Clara increased the number of dining chairs at the table and let in two additional guests each evening for a fee.

Being a clever and caring young woman, Clara convinced Arthur that it would be best for him to dine with the guests each evening.

"Arthur, it would be wonderful if you could help entertain the guests at dinner," she said. "Your presence will help engage the other locals to learn more about the inn, which may encourage them to commission your woodwork in the future," she added. Arthur thought that joining the evening meal with the guests was an excellent business decision.

Surprisingly, despite speaking so little with Clara, Arthur actively engaged in conversations with the inn guests and local diners. Occasionally, while Clara served their meals, she would hear Arthur discuss the war. Initially, these conversations were simple and usually sparked by interest in his Victoria Cross displayed on the mantel.

"Thank you for your service, lad," a guest would start. "You must have been quite a soldier to receive Her Majesty's highest honor."

Arthur would shyly respond, "War is a terrible experience, sir, and no one soldier should be honored above another. We were all very frightened at every moment, and the battles were chaotic and bloody. Every man present did his best to survive and to honor England. I am no better than anyone else who served."

Over the past few months, Arthur had begun speaking in a softer tone, accompanied by a slight rattle in his breath that Clara had observed. Despite this, he appeared happier than before, always looking forward to get back to his woodshop after brief dinners with the guests. Clara felt pleased to witness his gradual improvement in social interactions each day and hoped that every subsequent evening would bring even greater progress.

Arthur was becoming increasingly determined to create a special desk for his family and the inn. He reasoned that Clara could use the piece for managing the inn's finances and correspondence, and it could be passed down to his eventual heirs. He shared his idea with Clara, having settled on the design of a classic secretary's desk. Even Her Majesty owned a few that came from France. He concluded that an English secretary's desk for the inn was exactly what he needed for his next project and that he would secure just the right maple tree to create it.

Clara mentioned that there were some exceptional trees just beyond the inn's stone fence in Maplewood Meadow—the exact meadow where, just a few years earlier, she had seen Saint Martha.

Clara never mentioned this vision to Arthur, nor had Arthur shared his dream of Saint Martha on the battlefield with her. Nevertheless, he agreed to the inn's namesake when Clara suggested it. Perhaps if the two had communicated their visions to each other, there might have been a better understanding between them of what had transpired—but each kept their respective secrets to themselves.

The next day, an interesting conversation took place between the two at breakfast.

"Arthur, have you selected a tree for our family desk?" Martha sweetly inquired.

"Not yet, but I do feel that I am ready. I was going to go into the meadows today to choose one as I feel it is time to create our family heirloom," he replied in a slight whisper of a voice.

"Arthur, are you feeling up to it? I've noticed that you seem a bit tired. Perhaps I can take some time this morning and assist you with this task. I love the meadow so much and feel at home there. It would be wonderful for the two of us to choose the tree together since it will be for our family," she responded.

Arthur lit up when thinking about the two of them going to the meadow. He imagined their courtship before the war and how they felt so free, running together in the long green grass and resting in the shades of the many mighty maples.

Surprisingly, Arthur replied affirmatively: "Gather your things, and I will get the necessary equipment. It's time for us to create our future."

Clara smiled—at last, Arthur was returning to her from his inner wounds from the war.

Clara ran to the sewing shop and reassigned her apprentice to help with the inn duties for the morning, and the young couple went forth into the meadow to reclaim their peace.

It was truly a beautiful day in the meadow. The sky resembled the stunning stained glass at Clara's church. The grass was a brilliant green, and the trees were towering and bountiful.

Clara beamed in her newly made day dress, crafted from various leftover pieces of her many clients' frocks. It was an "everyday" version of the fashion of the day and fit her svelte figure perfectly. She silently thanked her mother for providing her with the skills to create such a beautiful—yet practical—ensemble from the bits and pieces of fine silks and trimmings from her customers. She had even added decorative bows to the sleeves, which matched perfectly with the wide skirt and petticoat beneath, all created from a stunning indigo-blue textured silk bolt she had found for her client.

As they quickly made their way through the meadow, Clara felt delighted to be with Arthur, who at that moment appeared healthy and strong. There was no sign today of the sadness that often consumed him or the labored breaths that typically burdened him. Perhaps all was finally well.

The tree selection took some time, with Arthur deliberating over several field maples from which to make the desk. Clara had decided that Arthur should pick a maple, and she would agree to any one that he thought appropriate. Her happiness did not depend upon the tree; rather, it was focused on seeing him vibrant and happy once more.

It was a hot day, so Clara told Arthur she would sit in the shade while he continued to choose the perfect maple tree for the desk. A bit farther away, she saw a large, full tree that seemed somewhat familiar. However, there were so many field maples in this meadow that she did not think twice about her premonition. Clara sat with her back against the shady tree and watched Arthur look here and there, realizing that he was having trouble finding just the right one.

She chuckled to herself at his perfectionist tendencies. He had always been remarkably focused and could master any task. Clara was simply relieved to see him enthusiastically engaged again, and watching him made her heart full. After hunting for the perfect tree for nearly an hour, Arthur came to Clara and sat under the maple with her.

"I simply cannot decide. They are all beautiful—majestic and bold. Each one would be wonderful for the desk, yet I don't feel as though the right one is here."

"Do you expect the tree to tell you to cut it down to make a desk from it?" Clara laughed. "I did not know that a tree would make such an intention be known."

"I can't quite explain this, Clara, but the right maple will reveal itself to me. This desk will be part of our family for centuries, so only the right maple will want to join us."

He wrapped his arm around Clara and gently kissed her forehead. As they melded into each other against the sturdy trunk of the maple, a strong breeze swept through the meadow. It had a strange, soft, yet powerful force that literally pushed them firmly against the maple's welcoming base. The tree felt warm, strong, and loving, like a part of them.

"This is the one, Clara. It's as if the universe pushed us to it." Clara had felt the energetic force as well.

"Arthur, I can feel it too. There is something awe-inspiring about this maple."

"Our decision is made," the two simultaneously said to each other, smiling—both unaware that they had just chosen the very maple that had concealed Saint Martha that day in the meadow.

And so, Martha's special maple would serve as their desk.

Arthur had long admired the fine craftsmanship used to make traditional secretary's desks. These desks originated in France, deriving their name from *secretaire*, the French term for "writing desk."

Best known as a tall, rectangular desk featuring dovetail joinery and velvet-lined drawers, the appeal of the secretary's desk lay in its numerous pigeonhole compartments and elaborately carved wooden columns concealed behind the signature drop-down panel that served as the desktop. The taller upper console of the desk included glass panels through which one could glimpse several shelves filled with cherished treasures.

Field maple, known for producing sturdy timber with a soft, rich brown color and silky shine, delighted Arthur, and he knew the special maple harvest of wood would be perfect for this family desk. He carefully planned the desk's completion schedule, knowing that the large, heavy piece would need a base of drawers, the hinged desk component, and the large bookcase on top.

Arthur was excited to design the piece and immediately began working on it. He had studied the masters of desk-making and was determined to create a unique piece for his family. He experimented with a process where he quartered each log, cutting it in the middle to create four spears and then sawing slices off for the boards. The process created a wavy grain orientation that Arthur thought was perfect for the desk.

Indeed, Arthur had become so enthralled with desk-making that he brought on a helper for his harp and other woodworking assignments. He simply could not stop imagining the desk, and he enjoyed every step of the process, feeling the wonderful maple in his hands as he patiently crafted each piece.

Working with this maple was astonishingly easy. The wood seemed to mold into any shape that Arthur desired. It felt warm to his touch as if it were alive. He reveled in its subtle shine and soft, comforting color. He had never worked with wood like this before.

Arthur's goal of completing the desk within half a year's time was coming to fruition, and Clara would go to the workshop with him each evening after dinner to check on his progress.

"This is magnificent, Arthur. This piece will be with our family for centuries, and all our children, grandchildren, and their children will feel your loving touch when they sit at this desk," Clara gratefully commented.

Arthur wrapped his arms around his beloved bride. "Clara, my heart and soul are in this piece, and I want to give it to you as a sign of my enduring love, and in thanks for yours in return."

Clara's patience had paid off. Arthur was returning to her bit by bit, day by day. The war was becoming a distant, blurry memory. She hugged him tightly in return and, for the first time, noticed how thin he had become. Perhaps he was not taking enough breaks within his day to properly eat his meals. She vowed that, from this day forward, she would ensure he was well-fed!

As Clara left the barn, Arthur took a deep, measured breath. He had been doing his best to keep her from hearing the rasp in his chest. The lingering cough he had endured for months seemed to drain so much energy from him.

Was it the many hours in the workshop? He did not know. But he knew that completing the desk was his mission now, and his health concerns could wait for another day. He wanted to present her with the final desk this Christmas as an offering of hope and love for the coming year.

The fall went by without event. Clara was busy with her inn guests and supervising her growing sewing business. She had taken on a second assistant to help with both the inn and the upholstery work; but she kept the pattern design as her own. Her innovative and flattering dresses, along with eye-catching draperies and bedding, were becoming well known throughout the area.

The tasks of sewing, upholstery, meal preparation, and cleaning the inn could be assigned to others. Arthur still joined the inn's guests for dinner each day, marking the only occasion he left his workshop, consumed by his self-imposed deadline to finish the desk.

The workshop was drafty, and Clara was increasingly worried about how much time Arthur spent in the barn, so she decided to bring in a local heating expert to help design a better system for the workshop and the inn.

The wood-burning stove at the inn would remain in the kitchen area, but all other areas would soon feature new hot water heating boilers to regulate the heat for the coming winter. In the past, Clara and Arthur would not have thought it possible to afford this, but with their three sources of income, it was not only feasible but also necessary for the comfort of the family, guests, and staff. Clara mused that perhaps the new heating system would also help with Arthur's lingering cough.

Christmas was upon them. The inn would close for the holidays so that Clara, Arthur, and their staff could all take a much-needed break. Although there was no snowfall this Christmas, the inn and their quarters were cheery nonetheless, with the festive decor Clara had created. The two looked forward to this week alone, which would culminate in a beautiful Christmas Day featuring a trip to church, a fine dinner for just the two of them, and the unveiling of the desk.

The sun shone brightly that Christmas morning. Clara jumped out of bed, eager to embrace the day with excitement and anticipation of what was to come. She felt just a little nauseous that morning, most likely from their delicious yet indulgent Christmas Eve meal of oyster soup, roast beef and potatoes, mince pie, and mulled wine.

Thinking of their lovely evening together lit Clara's face up with a smile. It had been the perfect night by the fire. Clara lovingly stroked Arthur's golden hair after he fell asleep with his head in her lap following dinner. He was so tired yet happy, barely able to keep his eyes open after dinner. Still, Clara was filled with so much love and joy that she didn't dwell on his fatigue.

After their Christmas Day activities, it was time to see the finished desk. Clara had not been allowed to visit the workshop recently as Arthur wanted the final piece to be a surprise. The two walked hand in hand to the workshop. Arthur slowly opened the door, and there, in the center of the workshop, was the desk, illuminated by a beam of sunlight streaming through the frosted windowpane above it.

"Arthur, this is a masterpiece. The wood is so graceful that it's almost too beautiful to be considered just a piece of furniture," Clara said admiringly. "The craftsmanship is incredibly intricate—distinctive and handsome yet understated and commanding. I feel as though this desk is almost whispering to me, luring me to come closer. I have never seen anything like this in my life."

Bright sunlight flooded through the window high in the barn's ceiling, enveloping the desk and the young couple, who were both lost in this moment of wonder. A glowing aura surrounded them and the desk.

Clara placed her hand on the wood and instantly felt a jolt of energy flow from the desk through her body. She ran both hands along the smooth wood of its tall sides; the impressive piece stood tall and proud, almost as if it were a living being.

She opened the opaque glass-paned cabinet doors that housed the three interior shelves, imagining the treasures she would place inside them. Next, she opened and closed the hinged desk panel, delighting in the many compartments where she would store her papers. Finally, she carefully drew out the three drawers perched above the clawed feet of the desk base. Each one would one day be filled with her family's most important memories.

The waves of the tree's timber created a striking pattern that she had never encountered before; indeed, Clara had never seen a desk like this. It was almost as if it were a mystical desk crafted from a tree that they had chosen together, a tree that perhaps had chosen them.

Clara finally moved her gaze from the desk to Arthur. Arthur's attention was transfixed on the desk; he looked at it as if he were seeing it for the very first time.

As Clara looked at Arthur, she chided herself. *How could she have allowed him to become so thin? How could she not have noticed how loose his shirt and pants were on him? When did he start having difficulty breathing when he spoke?*

"Arthur, I truly love this desk. I cannot thank you enough for the dedication and love you have put into it. You have worked so hard for so many months. However,

I can clearly see that you are exhausted by all this effort. It is my fault for not insisting that you see a doctor. Let's schedule an appointment after the holiday to have you see Doctor James. I'm sure it's just a lingering cough, but it might be time for some medicine."

Surprisingly, Arthur agreed.

CHAPTER 3

Believe

Hooping cough. Chin cough. Whooping cough. A disease that kills young children, not grown men. A disease with no cure, only treatments to soothe symptoms. Coughing spells, loud "whoops" from deep, harsh coughing fits.

"It often leads to bronchitis or even pneumonia and can sometimes be fatal," was Doctor James's alarming diagnosis.

Arthur had whooping cough, and a persistent case at that. Lately, he often found himself gasping for breath between the seemingly endless coughing fits. Clara would daily dissolve the salt of tartar provided by the doctor in boiling water. That was all there was to alleviate his misery.

With Christmas behind them, the cold winter was upon them. Arthur was weak but proud, and he still worked a few hours each day in his woodshop while Clara tended to the inn.

The first week of January, a new guest arrived at the inn. Will Warren was in from Prince Edward Island, one of the British territories in North America. Will was on a buying mission for his father's retail company and spent his days scouring the English and Scottish countryside for items that his fellow Brits abroad might enjoy.

Will had been told about a talented craftsman who might have some wooden instruments or furniture available for purchase at Martha's Meadowside Inn, so he booked himself at the inn for a week's stay to learn more.

"Good day, my name is Will Warren," the charming young businessman stated exuberantly, as he arrived. "I have heard through various channels that there is a fine woodcrafter here who may have some instruments for sale."

Clara looked up at the handsome man before her, who was about her age, perhaps a year or two older. He was dashing and outwardly considerate. This man was so different from Arthur—he was more rugged in build, with curly dark hair, and twinkling green eyes. His demeanor was confident and outgoing, and he appeared healthy, worldly, and strong. His presence was magnetic.

"Nice to meet you, Will. It is my husband, Arthur, who you will want to meet regarding his woodshop. He and his apprentice are working on quite a few fine pieces that are almost complete, and some may be available for sale. I'll bring you to his shop in the barn so you can discuss what you are looking for with him directly," Clara explained.

"I would be delighted to meet your husband. I plan to stay a week's time during this visit and am eager to learn more about any items that may be for sale which I can bring back to Prince Edward Island and Novia Scotia.

"Our store in Prince Edward Island sells many European pieces as our islanders often miss their homeland and love to have fine English, Scottish, and Irish wares for their homes."

What an interesting fellow this Will Warren appeared to be! Sailing across the Atlantic Ocean to collect pieces for those missing their original homeland.

"Please follow me," Clara said as she turned to Will to bring him to the barn, feeling a bit of color rush to her cheeks.

Arthur was in the wood shop, sitting on his workbench, staring at an almost complete wooden flute. He seemed distracted. His color was very pale, and his face looked weary as if the very task of breathing was a difficult battle.

Will warmly greeted Arthur. Seeing the two young men side by side was a bit shocking to Clara. When had she become so accustomed to seeing Arthur so gaunt and lacking in energy?

Will's boundless spirit lit up the shop. He complimented Arthur on his fine work and discussed what might be for sale and what he might be able to commission. Clara left the two to discuss business and wandered back to the inn to prepare dinner for the guests.

That night at dinner, Will entertained Arthur and the other inn guests with tales of his beloved homeland, Prince Edward Island. He often traveled the route between Prince Edward Island, Nova Scotia, and the "Boston States" of America and regaled the dinner guests with stories of these adventurous lands.

Will would book passage on a freight ship to England several times a year in search of items from England and the surrounding area to bring back to his family's store, which his father had founded. On this trip, Will would look for suitable goods throughout the English country-side and perhaps even Scotland before returning home in a few weeks' time.

On that first night after Will arrived, Clara mainly stayed in the kitchen, quickly serving the courses, and having little interaction with the guests. Once the meal was cleared, she sat at the desk to journal, recording everything that had transpired that day and keeping track of Arthur's declining health. Then, she headed straight to bed, dreaming of happier times.

As the week progressed, Will proved to be an excellent guest. At times, he would even rise from the table to help Clara clear the breakfast or dinner dishes, engaging in small talk and sharing more stories about his adventures.

Clara found herself laughing at his tales and enjoying his sheer love of life and adventure. Will made the inn seem exciting and helped her admire Arthur's work even more than she had in the past. At times, she almost felt like everything would turn out just fine—that her husband would soon recover, and they would have a new friend in Will.

At the conclusion of his stay, Will reserved a room for a second visit. He planned to return within the month, and Arthur would finish a few key pieces that he intended to purchase.

Clara was somewhat surprised at how she missed having Will's pleasant, positive demeanor at the inn. Each morning, he would greet her and the other guests with a booming "Good day!" and then engage everyone with questions, intently listening and learning from their conversation.

Dinners became even livelier, especially with the delicious wines Will brought to share with Arthur and the guests. Arthur felt a strong kinship with Will, as if he were a brother, and thoroughly enjoyed their evenings together.

"Will is very pleased with the instruments we are making, and he's requested quite a few more to purchase in the coming months," Arthur mentioned to Clara one afternoon when she brought him tea in the workshop. Although Arthur was pleased about the additional work—and income—his health was still deteriorating, and he looked exhausted in the afternoon light.

"Are you sure you can manage all this work? Perhaps you should consider hiring a second assistant to help with the new assignments . . . ?" Clara asked.

Arthur contemplated the idea and assured Clara he would see if he could find additional help. This pleased her immeasurably, as she was certain rest would help restore Arthur's health.

The next few weeks were gray and cold, mirroring the mood at the inn and the shops—as well as the atmosphere between Clara and Arthur. While Arthur's health seemed stable, he was by no means well. Perhaps they were all just adjusting to his lower energy levels. The inn remained busy, and both shops were bustling as well. Arthur and

Clara felt overwhelmed with work and collapsed into bed each night, utterly exhausted.

"Arthur, my love, how are you feeling? Your work is progressing very nicely, and I can see you take great pride in it. But are you pushing yourself too hard? Can your two helpers take on a bit more responsibility while you oversee them?"

Arthur considered this an excellent idea. He felt he was once again slipping away emotionally from Clara and wanted to be a more attentive and loving husband. He simply didn't know how—first, it had been the trauma from the war, and now the exhaustion from a chronic cough that often wracked his body in spasms. But he promised himself he would try harder, and the very next day, he came up with a plan.

"Clara, I know it's winter and cold, but what do you think about us going to the meadow for a stroll after lunch today? It would be lovely to be outside in the sunshine and see the dormant trees glistening with frost. I've been thinking about it quite a bit, and I believe fresh air might be good for my lungs."

Arthur did not have to ask twice. Clara loved the idea and bundled them both up after lunch for a leisurely stroll in the crisp winter air. They walked hand in hand to the meadow, both feeling hopeful.

That evening after dinner, Arthur stroked Clara's hair in bed. "Clara, I pray that soon you will be with child. I know it's what we both want, and I am so sorry that it hasn't happened as we planned. Someday soon, I feel we will be blessed." He nuzzled into her neck and almost instantly fell asleep.

Clara sat at the desk after breakfast the following day and journaled. She felt a combination of so many emotions. She was happy, sad, excited, and fearful. Her sentiments regarding Arthur and their future felt so uncertain.

She rested her head on the desk, feeling its comforting warmth, and sighed. She considered attempting a second novena to Saint Martha, this time asking for Arthur's return to health, but part of her couldn't bear the thought of being disappointed again. While her previous prayers to Martha had brought Arthur back to her, the man who returned was not the same one she had married before he went to war.

Clara sighed and closed her eyes, allowing herself to be a part of the desk and its stability. Just as she was dozing, Will bounded into the room, a week early, for his return.

"Hello there! Sorry to barge in while you are resting, but I managed to get back early and hoped that there was a room available for me at my favorite English inn!" he boomed with a broad grin. This man was incorrigible, and undeniably charming.

"Of course we have room for you, Will, and Arthur will be very pleased to see you at dinner tonight. He's even hired another assistant to help with all the items you have requested from the woodshop," Clara politely responded while fumbling through the desk for a room key.

"Very well! I will see you at dinner, and, Clara, please join us this evening for the meal. I am happy to help serve, and I've brought some wonderful wines from my recent trip to Italy. Let's all enjoy them together." With that, he grabbed the key to his room from Clara's hand and dashed up the stairs. No doubt about it; Will certainly felt at home here, Clara mused.

Clara found herself humming in the kitchen that afternoon as she prepared a more elaborate meal than usual. She smiled to herself, considering the menu and what she would wear that evening.

Recently, she'd finished a lovely pink satin dress made from the remnants of a beautiful bolt of fabric that one of her clients had brought in from Italy. From it, she crafted a magnificent skirt and bodice for the woman and sewed her own, less elaborate but still quite beautiful, dress.

Yes, the pink it would be. A pink dress made from Italian silk, lovely Italian wines, and a menu highlighting Italian cuisine this evening. Tonight, Clara would try her hand at making pasta, which she would toss with olives, capers, and breadcrumbs in an olive oil sauce she had learned about from a recent Italian guest.

She would serve pan-roasted chicken cutlets and a large, tossed salad with the meal. She excitedly set the table—even with a setting for herself—and ducked into their quarters to dress.

There were only two additional inn guests that night, so a total of five for dinner. The conversation was lively with Will holding court and explaining in animated detail his recent travels through Europe—most notably in the Lake Como area of Italy with its breathtaking views of the Italian Alps.

Arthur thoroughly enjoyed Will's tales and often chimed in with laughter and questions. Clara loved seeing Arthur so happy—he was vibrant this evening at the dinner table. His coughing fits were much less tonight, and he winked at her over dessert, stating that the wine cured all his ills.

Arthur, Clara, and Will had become a trio, Clara thought to herself. Each was happy to be with one another. Will had become a family friend, a close and trusted confidant, and a business partner who was helping Arthur sell his fine pieces.

On this trip, Will stayed for over two weeks, traveling throughout the countryside daily in search of unique items to purchase and sell back home at his family's store on Prince Edward Island. He would rise early and be gone all day but always made it back in time for dinner.

Clara found herself counting the hours until his return each day. Sometimes, she caught herself daydreaming about what Will was doing on his expeditions, but then she would quickly come to her senses and put such thoughts aside.

She had the inn, her shop, and her ailing husband to consider!

Was it that night at dinner when she simply glowed in the pale pink dress, her blonde hair tied back with a matching satin bow, the flush in her cheeks, the intensity of her crystal blue eyes, the easy laughter—is that when Will knew? Was it how Clara's gaze matched his so often during conversation? How she appeared so interested in him and his work; fascinated by Prince Edward Island and eager to learn more about the world beyond England?

Was it that very same night, as she savored the delicious Italian wine, captivated by the descriptions of beautiful Lake Como and Will's many travels—was that when Clara realized? Was it the way he praised her cooking skills? The way he made her feel beautiful, intelligent, and special? Was that when she experienced an attraction she hadn't felt since first marrying Arthur?

Had she imagined the current of electricity in her arm when Will accidentally brushed against her while they took the dishes into the kitchen after the main course? What was that invisible stream of energy between them— drawing her closer and closer—as they washed the dishes side by side?

Together, they brought out the dessert from the kitchen. Clara cut each piece of chocolate torta, and Will served it to Arthur and the two other guests. The reality of the situation seemed to take over, and both quickly returned to their traditional roles.

Once seated back at the table, Will was fully engaged in conversation with Arthur and another inn guest, this time drawing the conversation back to Arthur and his woodworking projects.

Clara looked across the table at Arthur and Will. One was so tired, lost, and succumbing to an invincible foe, while the other was a powerhouse of vitality, life, and laughter. It broke her heart. But her developing feelings for Will were hurting her even more. The guilt was overwhelming, almost suffocating. She feigned no interest in dessert and headed back to her desk and her private quarters, where she could close the door and close her mind to what had just transpired.

After a good night's sleep, in a dreamless state, Clara woke and knew what to do. She would avoid close encounters with Will and be even more devoted to Arthur. She could not hurt Arthur; even by a betrayal in her mind, if not her actions.

Clara immersed herself in her work, insisting on helping more in the sewing studio and then retreating to the kitchen to prepare food that she would not again eat with her guests.

After a few nights of this cloistered lifestyle, Will knocked gently on her office door after dinner. He and Arthur had just finished dessert, and Arthur had insisted on working further on his many commissioned pieces.

Clara was back in her small but beautifully decorated office, with soft floor-to-ceiling curtains and a matching upholstered desk chair. There, behind the chair, was the desk. It was entirely captivating; tall and grand—yet inviting.

Will was enthralled by the desk. Once he laid eyes on it, he longed to feel its distinctive waved wood panels and open its welcoming window-paned doors to see what was housed on the shelves within. How had Arthur created such a masterpiece in such little time? And what secrets, thoughts, and desires had Clara written in her journal sitting at this fine piece?

Clara smiled at Will's reaction to the desk. She instantly realized that the desk had worked its seemingly magical attraction on him. He appeared enchanted by it, just as she was. Will stood before her as she sat at the desk, placing both her hands on its frame as if holding on for dear life.

"Clara, if I didn't know any better, I would say you are trying to avoid me."

"Of course I'm not avoiding you!" Clara stammered a bit too loudly in a trembling voice. "I simply have too much work to do and haven't had time to socialize with our guests."

Will looked directly at her and held her gaze. She felt lightheaded, and her heart raced. Could he see that her entire soul was reaching out of her body toward him? Did he feel it, too, or was it just her imagination?

"Well then, if you aren't trying to avoid me, you will just have to help me with a project. Arthur isn't feeling up to the task, so he has requested that I select and fell a tree for him tomorrow. As you know the meadow best—would you please come with me to choose the right one?"

She nodded in agreement and looked down at the ground.

"Let's plan to head out around noon tomorrow, then. Have a nice evening, Clara."

And he was off.

It was another sunny day in the meadow, but this time it was just Clara and Will, with no Arthur to act as a buffer. She did not pack a lunch as she thought it would be unwise to linger on this errand with a man for whom she clearly had feelings—and whom she was struggling to resist.

Today, there was no delight in choosing a tree. Clara went straight to the nearest field maple at the entrance of the meadow and declared it the perfect choice. "I'll leave you to the task at hand," Clara said quickly before turning to leave.

"Wait one minute there!" Will exclaimed with a full grin. "Where do you think you are going? I may require a little bit of help here," he said with a chuckle.

Clara obliged and remained while he made the initial cuts and felled the tree. "Now that I know you are safe, you can bring the logs back to Arthur in a few trips," Clara declared as she backed away.

But the sun was so bright, the sky was such a deep blue, and the clouds were perfectly formed as she tentatively walked backward, away from him. She couldn't tear her gaze away from his eyes, and the brightness of the day made her vision hazy.

She suddenly felt the world go blank around her; dizziness overcame her—and then down she went. Will ran toward her and quickly helped her up, his strong arms around her back, carefully lifting her from the ground. At that moment, the tension between them became hypnotic.

They looked at each other, neither moving nor speaking. It felt as if they were being drawn into each other by a force far beyond them. Just as it seemed he might kiss her, he gently, deftly, pulled back from the spell.

"There you go, right back on your feet, Miss Clara. Let's make sure your feet stay firmly on the ground the next time you try to run from me," he said in a sweet, soothing voice.

"I'll meet you back at the inn," Clara whispered and moved away. Confused and ridden with guilt, she made her way back home.

From that moment on, Clara did her best to avoid Will. He soon left the inn for Prince Edward Island, this time without a definite return date set.

"It was all for the best," Clara rationalized to herself as she and Arthur bade him farewell.

Over the following few weeks, ever so quickly, Arthur was slipping away. He slept all day, struggling to breathe, and was barely able to sip the bone broth Clara would simmer for him daily. Nor would he eat the warm bread she would try to tempt him with, bringing it to his bedside, straight from the oven.

"Clara, my time is near," Arthur whispered one late afternoon as the sun began its winter sunset march. "I know you feel as though you will be alone without me, but you are strong and talented. I have given you this desk to serve as your stalwart guide. You will feel my love while you work there, writing in your diary and pondering what lies ahead. Do not despair; I will always be with you, just like the air you breathe. I will love you forever. Believe in yourself."

Like a bird taking flight, Arthur was here one moment . . . and then he was gone.

Time stood still, and before she realized it, March had arrived; spring was almost here. Clara sat at the desk and picked up her diary. Her tear stains had dried on nearly every page, blurring the pen entries to the point where she could hardly reread them.

Rereading them didn't matter. Each one felt the same. Clara was now a young widow, heartbroken, with an inn, a woodshop, and a seamstress business—all of which she could barely manage due to her malaise. Her staff were invaluable to her, helping her keep the business afloat as she slowly moved through her despair.

Clara had buried Arthur in a coffin made from the last of the special maple tree timber in the cemetery near the maple woods meadows. Her grief was overwhelming, leaving her with barely enough energy to get out of bed each morning. She was a widow without children, parents, or a reason to move forward, yet she dutifully greeted the inn guests each morning and during the evening meal, which were the only tasks she could manage for herself at that time.

Then, one day, he appeared. Will had come back to the inn after hearing from acquaintances about Arthur's death. He discovered Clara in her office, seated at her desk. His expression was filled with sorrow as he approached her. It seemed as though he could sense her thoughts, grasp her pain and fear. It felt like they had a connection from a previous lifetime, and he was there to rescue her. Will was prepared and willing to bear Clara's suffering.

Over the next few days, the two sat in silence during many meals. She was too saddened to speak, and he was too uncertain to declare his intentions. On the third day of Will's stay, he asked if they could take another stroll to the meadow. The days were longer now, and the sun was warmer. Perhaps they could bring a lunch and just talk.

Clara wore a dress made from green silk that day; a dress she had made to wear to church for Easter. She did not even bother to tie back her long blonde hair, and it flowed freely as she strolled the meadow, picnic basket in hand.

Watching the two of them from a distance, one might assume they were a couple, if unaware of the circumstances. They leaned into each other, sharing lunch and comfort. Their time together now felt different, calmer, and more intimate than before.

Clara was having a hard time finishing her meal; for the past few weeks, she had not been feeling well—the grief had taken so much from her. Will noticed her lack of appetite and asked what was wrong.

"I fear my sadness has robbed me of the joy of food," she replied.

The second week of Will's visit following Arthur's death began to feel different. They both mourned Arthur's loss, but they knew in their hearts that they had been losing him for quite some time.

At Clara's request, Will met with the woodshop assistants to discuss and plan for the various requests he had commissioned. The two apprentices were capable and eager to continue with the numerous orders. The sewing shop was just as busy as ever, as was the inn. Clara contemplated it all. She felt exhausted. Weary to the bone. How could she keep up this pace? After each dinner, she would sit at the desk and write about the day's events, always finding comfort there as Arthur had promised.

Will was deeply concerned about Clara's health. She looked pale and could barely keep any food down. He insisted that she immediately schedule a visit from the local doctor.

The doctor stopped by the next day while Clara was in the kitchen preparing the evening meal. "Clara, do you have a minute? I would like to talk to you about how you are feeling."

Clara brought him to her office, where he asked her about several health issues and conducted a brief examination.

"Clara, I do believe that you are with child, probably about three months along," he caringly stated. Clara began to cry. She felt weak and thought she might faint.

"Please take care of yourself. I understand you are grieving, but you need to rest and make sure to eat properly for the health of this baby," the doctor cautioned.

In disbelief, Clara thanked him for visiting, said her goodbyes, then locked herself in her office and sobbed.

"How can I raise Arthur's child alone with all this responsibility?" she cried to herself. Without any family to help, she felt so alone and isolated; the situation made her overwhelmingly despondent.

Will had just returned to the inn when he heard soft weeping coming from the office. He gently knocked and asked if he could come in to see her. She unlocked the door and collapsed into his arms, tears streaming down her cheeks.

"I am with child," she wept. "How will I be able to raise this child by myself and take care of the inn and the shops? I just don't know what to do!"

Will wiped away her tears and gently held her face in his warm hands.

"Clara, I know this may come as a shock, but I have never met a woman like you, and I believe I am in love with you. I understand that you are still grieving, but I would be honored if you would consider coming back to Prince Edward Island with me and starting anew there, creating a life for yourself and your child as my wife. I would love this child as my own and provide you with the security you need. Please consider my proposal."

He kissed her sweetly on the top of her head and left the room.

Clara could not believe what had happened. Yet she needed to believe in something or someone at this moment in time.

And believe she did.

CHAPTER 4

Hope

There was so much to manage before heading to Prince Edward Island, and for Clara, the morning sickness that extended relentlessly into the evening impacted her ability to carry out even the simplest tasks without becoming exhausted. Will and Clara had decided to sell the inn, as it was their most significant asset, but Clara's woodworkers and seamstresses could take on those respective businesses independently, perhaps even renting the current workshop spaces from the new inn owner. Now, the goal was to find a buyer and turn the plan into a reality.

Will had returned to Prince Edward Island several times since meeting Arthur and Clara. As the eldest son of a merchant family, Will had been traveling back and forth to England for many years. He loved the land where he was born, a British colony with a yearning for independence, and many island residents were also interested in the possibility of joining either the Canadian provinces or even the United States. Will's family's faith was Protestant, but Prince Edward Island also recognized the

Catholic Church, so he felt confident that Clara would find her spiritual home there.

Clara felt overwhelmed by the moving plans. Her heart ached as she contemplated leaving England. Her parents and Arthur were buried here, but they were all that she really had left in this country. Since childhood, Clara had always been busy with her family and their work, then followed the same pattern with Arthur. There had been little time for friendships or frivolity.

Part of her felt excitement about this adventure across the sea, while another part was filled with terror. What if Will's family didn't accept her? What if they discovered she was pregnant before marrying Will? Or that this baby wasn't his?

What if she were so homesick that she couldn't find happiness in this new land with her new husband? The questions spiraled endlessly in her mind.

"Will, what will your family think of me? They're going to meet a woman who is pregnant and from another country, whom you married so quickly without having met them. I'm nervous they might think I trapped you, and I understand how much they mean to you."

Will moved behind Clara, wrapping her in his loving embrace. "Clara, my family will love you just as I do, and even if they didn't, it wouldn't change my mind about marrying you or raising this child. Meeting you has brought me immense joy, and I am confident that we will have a long and happy life together."

His words meant the world to Clara. Now, she just needed to believe them.

Will decided a quick wedding in England would be the best solution to the issue of the forthcoming child. Since he was not Catholic, they were wed, as she had been to Arthur, in the Anglican Church of England. The ceremony was brief, with only the inn and shop staff in attendance. This time, Clara did not ask for her priest's blessing. Her guilt was too great to hide her pregnancy and her feelings toward Will, which had grown significantly since his proposal.

Part of Clara wondered if her intense feelings for Will stemmed from desperation; however, she recognized that he had ignited something within her the day they met at the inn. Will had a whimsical quality; he was funny and kind, adventurous and capable, strong and wise—and undeniably handsome!

Her physical attraction to Will was irrefutable. Clara lit up when he entered a room and relished lying in his arms, feeling his strong masculine energy. His extraordinary acceptance of her pregnancy was something she could never repay. Will appeared excited about the coming baby, gently kissing her burgeoning belly each morning and talking to the unborn child. How could she have been so fortunate to find a second wonderful man to love her—and her child?

Immediately after their marriage, Will set out to find a buyer for the inn. During his travels in England, he had met several businessmen, so it didn't take long for him to bring a few prospects for a visit and dinner. Clara had created such a warm and welcoming atmosphere at the inn that every initial impression was truly remarkable.

Clara had also been proactive in teaching her seamstresses about the operations of the inn—from general bookings to room cleaning and meal preparation. At this point, Clara felt confident that the inn would be in good hands with a new owner and that she could leave it with peace of mind. Part of her was fully prepared for the conclusion of this chapter and the beginning of the next in her and Will's life.

A gentleman from outside London offered Will a fair price for the inn after spending the night. He was also impressed by the woodshop and sewing studios and met with the staff, proposing a reasonable rent that would allow them to stay on. Both accepted happily, with promises from Will that he would return to continue commissioning work for both to bring back to his buyers in Prince Edward Island and Nova Scotia.

Now, it was time to pack the items they wanted to take to their new home and life across the sea. The most important pieces were, of course, the desk and its upholstered chair, but Clara also selected some of Arthur's creations from their personal collection, including a beautiful harp. The desk would need extra care during packing for the journey, which could take up to two weeks. Will had set a departure date for the following Monday, providing Clara only five days to complete her work and clear the desk of its current belongings.

Clara's heart was full—yet also broken.

One evening after dinner, she thought to herself, *How can I feel both emotions so deeply?* She wrote in her journal about her losses and her hopes for the future. Tomorrow, she would empty the desk and prepare it for packing, in preparation for her new life ahead.

The next morning, after breakfast, Will left for the day to solidify some additional items he was purchasing to bring back home. Clara had set aside the morning to pack up her materials from the desk—photos, her journal, ledgers, and notes—each an important part of her journey. As she carefully stowed these treasures, she took the time to read many notes and diary entries she had saved over the years.

Tears welled in her eyes as she reminisced about her early days of marriage to Arthur, rereading his deployment letter for the war and the numerous other correspondences he sent from the battlefield—each one filled with promise and hope, without dwelling on the horrors he was witnessing.

She discovered various letters her parents had saved, along with the death notices for both her mother and father. So much pain was concealed in the various compartments of this desk. Yet Clara understood that this moment of reflection was also an opportunity for healing. Once the desk was emptied of all its contents and carefully organized into boxes for the move, Clara sat back and admired this magnificent piece.

The desk was truly beautiful. The wood was unlike any other, showcasing a stunning river-like pattern in the maple. Arthur had crafted a masterpiece, and the warmth of this desk was incredibly inviting. Clara reached out to caress the wood, pressed her cheek against its side, and let the flow of energy—past, present, and future—stream into her soul.

She stood with her cheek pressed against the side of the desk for a few moments, almost embracing it as she let her emotions wash over her. Then, she slowly moved to the front of the desk to lift its writing panel for packing. At that moment, something caught her eye. Was that a small slip of parchment paper wedged in a crevice of the desk?

Were her eyes deceiving her? She had just emptied the entire desk. She felt behind one of the small compartments. The slot was empty, but a small piece of paper appeared to be sticking out from behind it. Clara carefully pulled the paper to avoid tearing it. The small note was actually a larger piece of parchment that had been meticulously folded into a square, about an inch in diameter.

Clara opened the paper. There, in his distinctive handwriting, was a note from Arthur, dated just a week before he passed away:

My Dearest Clara,

I know that I will not be with you when you read this note. My time with you was the happiest of my life. You are a remarkable woman, Clara. You have achieved so much, from taking care of your family to becoming a successful businesswoman—even if you didn't set out to be one—to being the most loving and loyal wife.

I know that it has not been easy to be with me these past years. The war took so much from me in terms of my physical health and the overwhelming thoughts of bloody battles. Yet, you stood by my side, comforting

and loving me. You have my support in whatever you choose to do next. Move forward with purpose and passion. Do not be afraid to love again. You deserve all the happiness that this life has to offer.
Your devoted husband, Arthur

Clara set the note aside. She was trembling, yet surprisingly not crying. She sensed Arthur's presence. He was with her now and would always be. It was time for her to move forward and embrace her destiny.

Clara decided not to tell Will about the note. The two were far too busy to dwell on anything except the journey ahead. Will had slowly been telling Clara all about his family.

Will's father, George, had sailed ships for years, bringing back goods to the "new lands" in North America. The family resided on Prince Edward Island, where he owned a large store in the main township of Charlottetown. Will had followed in his father's footsteps, spending years collecting goods from England, Scotland, and other European destinations to sell there.

He enthusiastically described his two brothers and two sisters, all of whom were married and living in Charlottetown. Each contributed to the store, which traded with the local Indigenous people and European settlers. It was a thriving family business, and all the Warrens played a role in it in some way.

Will described his father's larger-than-life personality to Clara. From Will's account, George Warren seemed like one of the most powerful men on the island.

Before entrusting Will with the traveling responsibilities, George had visited many countries and brought back numerous rare finds—from candlestick holders to tables and chairs, books, jewelry, and more. The items that were not sold to their customers were kept in large oak barrels in the attic above the family store.

Will's mother had passed away just a year ago, and his father continued to live in the large two-story apartment above the store where Will and his siblings were raised. Will had not mentioned his mother's death to Clara or Arthur, but now Clara understood that his private grief over her loss was compounded by his concern for his father.

Clara knew that she would have much to learn about her new husband's family and way of life. Having been so involved in business herself, she hoped that Will would see her as an equal once they set up their own home.

"Will, how do you feel about me helping with the store or perhaps offering my sewing services to your customers?" Clara asked a few days before they were due to leave on the ship.

"Isn't raising our child going to be a full-time responsibility for you? Will that be enough, or do you need some other activity as well?" Will inquired, not in a threatening manner, but rather as a question to which he knew there was no answer.

"I'm not sure. I have always had to work to help support my parents and Arthur. I know that, even though I no longer need to for financial reasons, I still enjoy it. Perhaps we can find a way for me to be both a mother and part of your endeavors as well."

Will looked at Clara and winked. "Clara, you are a woman who can do anything well, so we shall see what situations present themselves—or what ones you create for us." He chuckled. This woman was so unique, intelligent, and curious—how could he tell her what to do or not to do? His family would just have to get used to the firebrand he had married.

"Clara, there are many ways to contribute, and the island needs assistance in several areas. While our family may thrive, not everyone does, and there will be chances to help out. I promise we will make you happy in your new homeland," he said thoughtfully as he swept in and pulled her close for a kiss.

The boat journey was challenging. Clara felt perpetually unwell, and the constant swaying of the vessel as it crossed the Atlantic caused her daily bouts of nausea. Most of the time, she remained in bed in their modest quarters.

Merchant ships were far from luxurious, and many succumbed to the dangers of such long stints at sea. Clara had thought Will's travels were so glamorous; now she better understood that her new husband's position within the family business was one filled with responsibility and challenge.

Will never complained. He admired the captain and crew, always complimenting their skills. Will also grew up surrounded by the sea and had many friends who built and sailed on ships. If it weren't for his father's store, Will could have imagined himself as a ship captain.

Throughout the voyage, Will checked all the wares he had purchased and that were being transported below deck in the cargo hold. He also ensured that the desk and other items were properly secured and wrapped to prevent damage during their journey.

When they finally arrived at the harbor in Charlottetown, Clara was eager to see land—but incredibly anxious about meeting her new family. Thin from constant nausea, Clara did not appear pregnant, but her face lacked color, and her usually soft, wavy blonde hair was matted from the arduous journey and lack of proper nutrition due to her nausea.

She clung to Will tightly as they disembarked from the ship. Squinting in the sunlight, she spotted a small crowd of his Warren siblings and their children, along with Will's father, waving at them. Taking a deep breath, Clara waved back with all the energy she could muster.

The Warren family was certainly a lively group. Will, the eldest of the clan, was quite the eligible bachelor on the island at twenty-six years old. Before her passing, Will's mother had beseeched him to marry soon.

"Will, with all your traveling and the responsibilities of your father's business, it would be wonderful for you to have a partner to share this life with. I know you say you haven't met the right woman yet, but perhaps you're being a little too selective. The heart can grow to love a loyal and caring companion."

Little did his mother know that, over the past few months, Will had indeed found the woman he had been seeking; however, she happened to be married to another man in a different country.

But now was the time for celebration. Will and his new bride, Clara, had arrived on the island and the family had a new member to get acquainted with.

Before their journey, Will and Clara decided not to inform the family about her previous marriage, and certainly not about the paternity of the child in her belly—her pregnancy would be another secret they would unveil in due time.

"Clara, how did you meet Will?" "What did you do before marrying Will?" "How did your family feel about your move to Prince Edward Island?" "Will they come to visit?" The Warrens' questions came fast and furious. Thankfully, Will and Clara had well-rehearsed answers for each.

After explaining that Clara's parents had tragically passed away and left her an inn in a small English village, the story of meeting Will as an inn guest became a captivating tale of love at first sight.

No mention was made of Clara's seamstress shop, the woodworking studio, or Arthur. The story was swift and effective—and everyone seemed completely satisfied with it. The family felt at ease with Will's explanation about his assistance in selling the inn once they decided to marry. He apologized for their quick nuptials in England, but they were so in love that they simply could not wait. The

Warren family expressed enthusiasm about planning a family celebration on the island within the week.

Will also made it clear that Clara was definitely not a woman who married their brother for money, as she had inherited property. No mention was ever made of Clara working in the inn or the shop—these details were quickly overlooked.

Everyone gathered around Clara and chatted endlessly while the couple waited for their luggage—and the desk. Two of Will's brothers brought a wagon to help load the desk and their travel trunks. Then, they all formed a caravan to Will's home, just a few miles from the harbor.

Will had purchased his own house a few years earlier. It was in the popular Maritime Vernacular style, which resembled a cottage. The front entrance had small windowpanes on either side of the front door, and a second-floor window allowed sunlight to shine through into the main part of the home.

The house had been built only a decade earlier, and Will was its second owner. Clara thought it was the most charming house she had ever seen.

Will feigned exhaustion and the need to get settled instead of meeting the entire family that evening for dinner at his father's home. There would be plenty of time for family celebrations, and his sisters had left them a delicious homecoming meal, which was exactly what they needed.

After years of living in century-old buildings, Clara could not wait to explore her new home. She was equally excited to create beautiful window curtains, bedding, and upholstery for this charming house that needed a bit of feminine care. But her most important mission now was to find just the right spot for her beloved desk.

Completely in love with his new bride, Will picked Clara up and carried her into the house upon their arrival. Today, he wanted to help Clara settle into her new life. He hoped she would love it here as much as he did. He also wished he could help her move past the sadness of her past and embrace her new future on Prince Edward Island.

It was spring, and Clara felt the earth awakening in this beautiful new land. Prince Edward Island was different from England in many ways but similar in others. The rolling hills and meadows resembled her previous home, although the variety of trees here was distinct from her beloved Maplewood Meadow. Instead of field maples, there were sugar maples and red maples. Will hinted that these trees would be quite glorious to behold when the fall foliage arrived.

The pastoral landscape was framed by the island's coastline with its many bays, coves, and small inlets. Red sandstone cliffs stood tall over white sand beaches. A small island with a relatively small population, Prince Edward Island was indeed beautiful, and Clara enjoyed taking in the robust sea air.

Will and his brothers all worked in the store with their father, some handling the finances, others stocking shelves and tending to customers. Will's primary role was purchasing goods—particularly home items—mainly from England, Scotland, and Ireland, but there was talk of heading to other areas more regularly as well.

Shipbuilding was vibrant at the time, and the island's economy depended on trade with its neighbors in the Americas and overseas. Will was friendly with many of the shipbuilders and captains, and he and his father would often converse with them about new countries to visit for trade and procurement opportunities.

Clara truly enjoyed getting to know her new brothers- and sisters-in-law and their many children, but she especially cherished her new father-in-law, George. George Warren was a rugged man with a big heart that had been broken by the recent loss of his wife. Thankfully, he had a supportive and loving family around him during this time. He never dined alone and was constantly surrounded by his children, their spouses, and his grandchildren, most of whom lived nearby and worked alongside him in the family business.

Clara immediately took up sewing again. The store had many bolts of interesting fabrics that she could use to personalize the house. She made curtains and bedding and reupholstered the sofa and chair.

Will was amazed by how she had transformed his house into what could now only be described as a true home. After a long day at work, he would return to find Clara in the kitchen, preparing her favorite dishes from her time at the inn. The house sparkled with its new decor, and at the focal point of the living room stood the magnificent desk—as if holding court over the house and its inhabitants.

"Clara, it's wonderful to see you so happy and healthy, and I truly believe that the baby is starting to show," Will beamed at dinner. "I think it's time to announce our new child's arrival to my family."

A bit reluctant to do so, Clara responded, "Oh, Will, I've just been here a month. Can't we wait just a bit longer? I don't want your family to feel as if you were forced to marry me!"

"Well, the baby is expected this fall, so we need to tell them soon, even if we feigned that this child arrived a bit early. We can wait a few more weeks, but I'd like to inform everyone by my father's birthday." The decision was made; the announcement would be made on May 1.

As promised, on the first of May, Will and Clara hosted a celebratory dinner at home for George's birthday. Clara prepared delicious, slow-roasted chicken, accompanied by her famous crispy potatoes and root vegetables. The meal was delectably concluded with a special English pudding. Will made a toast during dessert, thanking his family for welcoming his bride, and then announced the news that they would soon be a family of three.

All the Warrens applauded, delighted with the news. There was no mention of the forthcoming timing of the birth, just general happiness that Will had found his person and was completely happy.

Will did not travel all summer; instead, he met regularly with one of his younger brothers to start teaching him about traveling and purchasing. Will had no intention of leaving Clara during the pregnancy or birth, and although he never mentioned this plan, she knew in her heart that he wanted to be there to protect her.

The season changed, and the sugar maples—and other foliage on the island—put on their glorious display. Clara marveled at the colors, which were perfectly offset by the bright blue sky, the sea, and the red clay of the cliffs.

Soon after September turned into October, the baby was born. He was a fair-haired, blue-eyed child who resembled Clara—or, as she pondered, Arthur. Will was thrilled to have a son, and the couple named him Christian Arthur Warren.

Will told his family that the baby was named after Clara's late father as a tribute to him. The secret was theirs to keep, and Will and Clara could not have been happier or more content in their new roles as parents.

Clara and Will loved their life on the island. Will's younger brother now helped with the sea travel component of Will's role in the family business, which allowed him to spend more time on the island with Clara and Christian. George Warren was delighted to have all his children around him and was pleased that his oldest son, Will, had finally found a perfect match in Clara.

Having no real family of her own, Clara melded beautifully into the Warren clan. She enjoyed the near-constant family gatherings, trips to the store, and entertaining the family at their home. Her years as the mistress of the inn had taught her how to prepare meals for larger groups, and the family frequently complimented her cooking. Her decorating skills were also admired, and she felt gratified by her sisters-in-law's requests for help with their impeccably designed curtains and upholstery for their own homes.

Baby Christian was a true wonder to her! He possessed an almost angelic appearance and nature. As ever-doting parents, Will and Clara's love for each other grew stronger every day, and their family life was fulfilling. It was more than Clara could have ever dreamed of; she could hardly believe that this handsome stranger, Will Warren, had entered her life and completely transformed it.

By her past standards, their life was both uneventful and joyful. There were always interesting people to meet at the store, including the Indigenous people who also traded there. Will's father was well known throughout the North American British colonies as a fair businessman with a keen eye for unique wares—and he stored many of his personal treasures in his prized oak barrels in the attic. No one really knew what was inside those barrels, but George promised to unveil these prized possessions as the grandchildren grew older.

Christian had a slew of cousins, and by the time he was two, he was quite verbal and playing well with many of them. Clara discovered on his second birthday that she was pregnant again—she and Will were thrilled when the doctor informed them. Six months later, a brother for Christian arrived.

This time, the baby had a full head of dark, curly hair and green eyes, just like Will. Clara was surprised by the differences in the appearances of the two boys but made no mention of it. Will now had two sons—each as import-ant as the other in his and Clara's eyes. They named their second son William, but he would be called Bill to avoid confusing him with his father.

Over the next decade, Clara and Will became active members of their community on Prince Edward Island. These years were a time of vast change on the island. Shipbuilding flourished for many years as the top industry, but the islanders also wanted a land route for travel, especially during the cold winters, so they embarked on a massive railroad project.

The construction of the railway had devastating consequences for the islanders, nearly bankrupting the local economy. In response to mounting railway debt—and an unfinished railroad—the island eventually negotiated to join the Canadian Confederation, becoming the seventh province of the North American nation.

During these years, Will's father gradually stepped back from the family business, allowing his capable children to take over, with Will as the leader. George had met a widow at church and now enjoyed a lovely companion who made his days infinitely happier. Clara had never been busier; she and Will now had five children under ten years of age—three boys and two girls. Christian was the only true blond-haired sibling, but two of the other children had blue eyes like their mother and light brown hair that easily became sun-streaked in the summer.

Clara and Will became engaged in local efforts to assist the less fortunate, donating excess goods and items from the store to various families. Over time, people from all over the island came to the back of the store to meet with Clara, and she would donate what she could to help those in need. These small acts of kindness nourished Clara's soul, and she couldn't believe her life could be so full and happy with Will Warren.

When Christian was thirteen, Clara and Will received the surprise of their lives—Clara was pregnant again with their sixth child. Adeline Edna Warren joined the family when Christian was fourteen. "Addie" was a dynamo. Right from birth, the spirited baby girl made her presence felt and would become her mother's sidekick, rarely leaving her side and eager to learn everything Clara knew.

It truly felt like a miracle. Clara sat at her desk and journaled. She wanted to thank Saint Martha for her life today. Though it was not exactly what she had prayed for all those years ago, her prayers had been answered in many ways. Arthur had been saved from the war, and his child now thrived. She knew Christian would have a special place in this world because of both his fathers' love.

Once an only child, Clara was now part of a large, thriving, extended family. Her family of six vibrant children was more than she could have ever imagined. Her marriage to Will was the greatest achievement of all. Together, they were partners in everything—from family to business to charitable work—while overseeing and guiding their children to have kind hearts and big visions.

The novena prayer recited years ago was not entirely answered—but Clara's life was just as it should be. She looked up from the desk, through the window, and into the clouds, thanking Martha.

At that moment, the clouds parted, and a beam of intense sunlight flooded through the window, enveloping Clara and the desk in its brilliance. Warming her face—and her heart—the sunbeam soothed her soul, heralding that she was now, indeed, home.

CHAPTER 5

Mysteries

Adeline "Addie" Warren was the last of Clara and Will's six children. She was the counterpart to her oldest brother, Christian, a thoughtful and soft-spoken young man who carefully chose his words and always pondered a question before responding. Although they looked nothing alike—Christian with his slender build, almost white-blond hair, and pale blue eyes, and Addie with her round face, curly to the point of unruly dark brown hair, and jade eyes—the two formed a strong bond almost immediately. Christian was always more than happy to assist his parents with his little sister, who was fourteen years his junior.

All the children, except for Christian, had inherited Will's boisterous and never-ending enthusiasm. Christian took his responsibility as the oldest child very seriously and was contemplative and watchful. He made it a point to always know where his siblings—Bill, John, Emma, Louise, and Addie—were so he could assist his parents in any way possible.

Clara could hardly believe that Addie had been born. What a surprise for her and Will—but the most pleasant one at that! Each of their children was so similar yet so different: Christian, with his calm and thoughtful demeanor; Bill, the spitting image of Will; John, a look-alike to his brother Bill with a tad quieter demeanor; Emma, the first sister after three brothers, with a strong voice; Louise, a quieter child who loved sewing and fashion; and then Addie, the baby of the family, six years younger than her closest sister, who was certain to be her own person.

All the children—except for baby Addie—attended the recently opened Wesleyan Day School, which had hundreds of students across more than a dozen classrooms. The school was celebrated for its innovative practices, including music classes for students and the expansion of the town library with a branch there.

Clara marveled at the teachers' mission to bring such excitement to learning. Music had always soothed her, and she remembered fondly the beautiful harps that Arthur had crafted years ago in the woodworking studio at their inn in England.

Long ago, Clara had packed up one of the smaller harps to bring to Prince Edward Island. Will had stored it in his father's attic next to the oak barrels that held so many treasures. She made a note to herself to have Christian find it for her.

"Well, who would have guessed that our attic held a world-class harp hidden away?" Christian exclaimed having just brought the instrument home after visiting his grandfather. It was so far back in the attic that it took

Christian quite a while to sift through the many other artifacts to find it.

"Mother, look how you wrapped it before you came here! It's packaged in this old, pale blue silk fabric, and all the strings are completely unscathed from your long trip. It's beautiful, and the workmanship is so well done. Where did you ever find this harp?"

Clara chose her words carefully; in her excitement about bringing the harp to the children's school, she had not realized how she would explain Arthur's craftsmanship.

"A nice woodworker in the village allowed me to purchase it years ago for the inn at a very fair price. I considered learning to play it, but I never found the time."

No further explanation was necessary; the children were too excited to look at the harp and imagine how to play it.

"Perhaps the music teacher at school will know how to make this harp sing." Will smiled as he held this meaningful piece in his hands. "It is lovely that your mother remembered this piece, a special tribute to her past, and let's see if we can make it part of this family's present as well." And with that, he kissed Clara's cheek and gave her hand a warm squeeze.

"Let us bring it to the school and find a harp player," Will boomed with his trademark grin as he directed the family toward the dinner table.

The next day, Clara brought the five older siblings, along with young Addie in tow, to the school. Christian led the group carrying the harp into the school, still wrapped carefully in the blue silk from England.

The Warren family was a well-regarded group in town, and their popularity at school was equally strong. As the township's most prominent shopkeepers, merchants, and philanthropists, Will and Clara, along with their children, were widely recognized.

Clara, now in her early forties, was as beautiful as she had been in her twenties. She was slight of frame yet athletic, walking with a bounce in her step. Her long blonde hair—which she often wore down in ringlets or pulled back around her face—still shined, and her complexion appeared to glow.

Clara continued to design and sew the family's garments, blending the fashions of her past in England with the newer styles seen on the island. With a strong sense of self, Clara crafted her garments from unique fabrics sourced from Will's brother's trips abroad. She appreciated fabrics that were comfortable and easy to move in, refusing to conform to the discomfort of contemporary fashion—which often involved high-collared necklines, impossibly tight sleeves, impractical bustles, and excessive underskirts.

Indeed, Clara stood out as she walked toward the school this day in her simple pale yellow dress, adorned with white lace details on each sleeve—a dress she had crafted to be practical for a mother of six. The dress reminded her of one she had made in England, which she wore while wandering through the meadows near the inn.

Once all the younger children were taken to their classrooms, Clara, Christian, and baby Addie made their way to the music room with the harp. There, Miss Henderson sat preparing her daily lessons for her class.

"Good morning, Miss Henderson," Clara warmly greeted their teacher. "I have a little surprise from England for you."

Clara acknowledged Christian with a nod while holding Addie in her arms. Christian entered the classroom respectfully, carrying the large instrument concealed under a wrapping of blue fabric.

"Ah, but what is this, Mrs. Warren?" Miss Henderson asked as she looked at the large item engulfed in its protective "jacket" of worn silk.

"Please feel free to see for yourself. It's a beautiful piece that has been hidden away in our family attic for far too long," Clara replied with a gentle smile.

The silk wrapping came off easily, revealing the magnificent harp shining in the sunlit room. For a moment, it almost took Clara's breath away. All those years, she had been so focused on the wonderful desk Arthur had created for her that she had forgotten about the many other exquisite pieces he had made.

The harp was simple in design but was made from a wood that looked oddly familiar. No, it couldn't be . . . Had Arthur crafted this smaller-scaled harp from that special maple? She didn't recall him mentioning that, but then again, at that time, she was in a different frame of mind, burdened with so much responsibility and a husband who was very ill.

"Do you know how to play the harp, Miss Henderson, or do you know anyone who might be able to? I would love for this piece to receive the attention it deserves."

Miss Henderson, a thoughtful young woman in her early twenties, grew up on the island but attended music school in Quebec City for two years. She returned home when the school opened and was recently hired as the new music teacher—a position she had only dreamed of in the past. She was a kind teacher with a deep knowledge and love of music that resonated in her soul.

"Coincidentally, Mrs. Warren, I learned to play during my training!" she exclaimed, her long fingers gliding over the wood of the harp. "The wood used to craft this piece is so interesting; do you know anything about its origin?"

"No, unfortunately I do not. Only the woodcrafter would know for sure."

Clara smiled secretly, as she now believed what she had once thought was impossible. The harp was made from the mystical maple and had long been hidden away. It was time for it to shine and spread its joy to others.

The Warren Harp, as it was referred to at school, was truly an instrument of wonder. Most children knew about the violin and enjoyed classical music, as well as "fiddling," which was always a more casual favorite. The harp, however, was a grander and more elegant string instrument that the children were instantly drawn to—especially the Warren Harp, with its beautiful carvings and vibrant wood.

Miss Henderson could make the harp practically sing when she played it, and the children were captivated each day as she shared more of the rich history of harp playing. She would then choose various pieces from different eras to perform for them.

Of all the Warren children, Christian was the most

taken with the harp. After each music lesson, he would feel its smooth frame gently with his hands, absorbing its history with every loving stroke of his palm.

What was it that attracted him so much to this piece? He asked his mother, the guardian of the family's English secrets, for more information about it.

"Mother, this harp is so different from the other musical instruments. I feel alive when I hear it played; I can see colors more vividly, feel content to my bones, and happy in my heart when it is played," he told Clara after school one day. "I feel as though it's a part of me that was missing, and I cannot get enough of its beauty and unique spirit—if one could think of an instrument as having a soul."

"Christian, this harp is something I cherished from my past and stored away in Grandfather's attic until I felt strong enough to see it again. I left England in despair, and your father rescued me from my lonely life after my family passed away. Now that we have once again brought the harp into the world, I feel so proud to be part of its past and its future. It is truly a gift to have it back in such an important way."

Christian sighed as he lovingly gazed at his mother. She had endured so much before his birth—losing her family, leaving her homeland, and starting anew on the island. He knew that his parents had a strong and loving marriage, yet he also recognized that there were secrets about their past that they kept. Nevertheless, he loved his mother with all his heart and believed that anything she withheld from them was for the family's best interests.

As Christmas approached, Miss Henderson organized a holiday musical concert for the students and their parents. Clara and Will were thrilled to attend with their five students and little Addie, each dressed in their holiday best, crafted by their mother. Will proudly secured seats in the second row of the auditorium on the evening of the concert.

It was only four o'clock in the afternoon, yet it was already dark outside, and the room was elegantly illuminated by lanterns for the musical performances. There were holiday sing-alongs, with attendees thoroughly enjoying the festive spirit. As the evening came to a close, the final solo performer took the stage. It was Miss Henderson, dressed entirely in white, seated in front of the harp.

The instrument and its player shone like a singular incandescent vision as she began to play and sing:

> *What Child is this who, laid to rest*
> *On Mary's lap, is sleeping?*
> *Whom angels greet with anthems sweet*
> *While shepherds watch are keeping?*
> *This, this is Christ the King,*
> *Whom shepherds guard and angels sing,*
> *Haste, haste, to bring Him laud,*
> *The Babe, the Son of Mary!*

Tears streamed down Clara's face as she listened to the angelic sound of the beautiful voice and magical harp. The song reminded her of England, her parents, and of

Arthur—of all that she had lost. Yet, as she looked into Will's eyes, she saw the depth of a love like no other.

This man had brought her here and helped her make a home. Together they were raising six children, the loves of her life. The enchanted harp continued to cast its spell on the auditorium. As the concert concluded and Miss Henderson finished the last loving words of the ballad, the crowd erupted in applause.

And then the most miraculous event of the evening unfolded before them all—a light, seemingly from above, brightly illuminated the entire harp and the strings in Miss Henderson's hands. There was complete silence in the room.

The harp's strings glowed with a heavenly golden hue. Miss Henderson gazed down at her hands resting on the instrument, her expression one of sheer awe. Everyone understood that they had just experienced something beyond this realm.

Clara wept tears of joy, and Will knew at that moment Arthur was also there with them, his glorious harp shining bright.

The school year passed without incident, and Clara and Will continued their many activities in township and provincial affairs. Clara began to assert herself for women's voting rights. She often laughed to herself, thinking that thousands of miles away from her home in England, she was taking a stand for equal rights with men when she had spent her entire early life working just as hard as they did! Curious times, indeed, she mused.

As the baby of such a large extended family, Addie always was entertained by the goings-on of her parents, siblings, aunts, uncles, and cousins. She could poke around in the store for hours while her parents worked, helping Clara sort through the charitable items for donations.

Her two older sisters were already interested in the fashions of the day and had embraced Clara's love of sewing, creating their own dresses for school and birthday parties.

Addie was just a bit too young to engage in any activities that didn't involve her mother. She simply adored being with Clara and was affectionately known as the "little shadow." Her favorite time of day was joining her mother at the desk—in the early years on Clara's lap, but later at her own little chair that was just the right height with a pillow.

"Momma, can I sit with you today and write at the desk?" Addie would begin each morning. "I almost don't need my pillow to write now!" she would playfully say. Addie loved writing in her own journal, initially featuring basic drawings but later focusing on spelling words, just as her mother wrote each day in her special notebook.

Addie knew her mother looked forward to her quiet time each day at the desk, and she never missed an opportunity to be with her, listening to the story of the special tree that had been used to create it. Clara had long modified the story to include her selecting the tree and having a local woodworker build the desk for her to use at the inn.

During her years on the island with Will, Clara softened her views on her Catholic upbringing and acquiesced in raising the children in the Episcopal Church. Addie and her siblings were all brought up in Will's church, which had also become an integral part of Clara's spiritual life. Clara and Will were regular attendees, enjoying the sense of community that their weekly visits offered them and their children.

The six Warren siblings enjoyed a wonderful upbringing on the island, where they had the freedom to explore the rolling hills, red-sand beaches, and rocky bluffs. Exciting activities were always around every corner, and the Warren children embraced every aspect of the adventurous life available on Prince Edward Island.

Will's father was now in his "golden years," as his children would call it, and Addie delighted in spending time with her grandfather. Clara would take Addie to visit a few times a week, and the two would explore the old oak barrels in the attic, rummaging through Grandpa's treasures.

"Grandpa, what was it like to sail across the sea and visit the old lands?" Addie would constantly ask. "Please tell me stories of what it was like back then. Did my father travel with you? How did you find these beautiful items? Were they expensive? Who owned them? Why did they sell them?" she would implore.

Grandpa George would chuckle and say, "Oh my dear Addie, you are such an inquisitive child and so curious about the world. Hopefully, one day you will explore it as your father and I have done. Perhaps you will even visit England, where your mother was born." He would then share even more delightful adventures with her as she perched on his lap.

The other five Warren children were now too old and occupied with school, friends, and chores to spend much time with Grandpa. Clara was glad that Addie brought him so much joy, as she did for Clara as well. While Addie loved her parents, grandfather, and siblings, her favorite was Christian, who was always eager to entertain her whenever Clara was busy.

As the years passed, Clara and Will determined that Grandpa might need someone to live with him in his home above the store. Christian was more than happy to oblige and seamlessly moved into an empty bedroom, located on the main floor, and assisted his grandfather with daily chores and keeping an eye on him as he went up and down the stairs, insisting that he did not need his cane!

Christian admired Grandpa's strong spirit and love for life, and he equally relished the captivating stories George shared about his life as a settler on the island and his numerous adventures back to the "homeland."

Clara and Will had their hands full with the constant comings and goings of their busy children, the business, their charitable work, and Will's father. Clara could hardly believe how much her life had transformed—transitioning from being an only child in England to a young pregnant widow, to now being the matriarch of this large, loving, and exciting family.

"Will, I can't believe the life you've given me here on Prince Edward Island," Clara whispered as she rested her head on Will's shoulder in bed. "It's more than I ever thought possible."

"Well, my sweet wife, the moment I saw you, I think I fell in love with you—even though I knew I could never have you since you were already spoken for. The turn of events with Arthur's sad passing was an act of fate beyond our control. I put my faith in the divine and am so happy that I could bring you here and build this family with you." Will nuzzled into Clara's hair. "It has all been a miracle for both of us."

Clara and Will understood that the love they shared should never be taken for granted, and they both appreciated their past, present, and hopes for the future. Together, they were stronger—anything seemed possible.

Will greatly enjoyed overseeing the store and watching his children grow into fine young adults. He often thought about how he had waited to meet the right woman for him, as his parents chided him for being so slow to find his match. Yet, he always knew in his heart that he could only marry for love—not just for a partner, not merely to have a wife, and not simply to have children. He valued and sought a love that was meaningful; his relationship with Clara began in a complicated way, but now it was solid and strong, transcending the bonds of parenthood. Will truly loved Clara, and she loved him in return. For him, it was his first love; for her, a second truly profound union.

One night, after enjoying a brandy by the fire, Clara and Will found themselves alone, the children fast asleep.

Will glanced up from his book and noticed Clara journaling at the desk. What was she writing? Will never asked and never sought to find out. He understood that Clara cherished her memories of the past but held a deep love for her present.

This one evening, curiosity overcame him, and before he could stop himself, he simply asked, "Clara, do you think of Arthur often? Do you see him in Christian?" Silence filled the air. Had he opened Pandora's box?

"Yes, Will, I do. I think of him, especially when I sit at this desk. I remembered him when the harp lit up that evening, and I see him every day when I look at Christian."

Will did not know how to respond. Had he hoped she had forgotten Arthur? Did he have the audacity to believe that he could overpower her emotions from her past?

"I think of Arthur with deep love and respect, and I know he is happy for me—and Christian. I believe it's possible to love again, and I have found that love with you, my dear Will," she whispered as she moved closer to him in his chair. Clara slipped her arm through Will's and guided him to their room.

The two never spoke of Arthur again.

The years passed peacefully as Will and Clara cherished their family, numerous friends, and their role in island society. They were natural leaders, and many islanders sought their counsel on various matters. Their charitable work was recognized throughout the community, and they took pride in raising their children with the same deep moral commitment to helping the less fortunate.

"We have so much, while many have so little. It's our duty to help those in need," Will would say at family dinners. "How have you helped others?" he would ask his children. The answers were sweet and kind. "Pa, I shared part of my lunch with a girl at school this week because she did not have enough and was still hungry," Emma beamed.

"I helped Mrs. Nee gather the apples that had fallen in her yard," John replied proudly.

Each child, regardless of age, was challenged to be a beacon of hope, and all were more than happy to rise to the task.

Christian never declined when their mother asked him to take Addie to the store while she attended local meetings. He was a devoted caretaker to both his younger sister and his grandfather. When Clara was away, Addie became his "little shadow," and he cherished every moment of her bubbly personality and endless questions.

With the children either at work or school, Clara and Will had much more time for their other interests, mainly helping the island community's economy and general way of life. The island had suffered setbacks over the years, including the crash of the shipbuilding industry, which employed so many islanders. As a result, more and more families needed to find employment off-island and were leaving for other provinces and the "Boston States" of America, where work was more plentiful.

Determined to keep the Prince Edward Island population vibrant, Will and Clara joined the new tourism initiative. This campaign aimed to attract other Canadians and Americans to visit Prince Edward Island during the warmer months as a vacation destination, enticing them with visions of the island's stunning landscape, white sandy beaches, and striking red rock cliffs.

Clara enjoyed assisting with the campaign, offering ideas for tourism, such as promoting travel to the island by ship or rail. The campaign even expanded to reach out to those recovering from illness, touting Prince Edward Island as the ideal place to recuperate with its crisp sea air, fresh farm produce, and daily-caught fish in the pristine coastal waters.

As tourism began to take off, the island government realized that adequate lodging was needed for these visitors. Soon, small boardinghouses and inns began to spring up on the island, and Clara, based on her prior experience as an innkeeper in England, was more than happy to consult with owners. Will was proud that Clara found meaningful activities for herself and that she had grown to love the island as much as he did.

The Warren family was content. Clara and Will felt blessed by the life they had created together and looked forward to the future, hoping that their children would marry and eventually fill their home with grandchildren. But for now, they still had a few children—most notably Addie—to finish raising.

Will and Clara were busy parents who had taken on many different causes that were important to them and their community. As they became more involved, Addie became further attached to Christian. She would come home from school each day and head straight to the store, where Christian would make her lunch and discuss her day with her. He looked forward to their time together each day and kept her busy helping arrange items in the store in the afternoon.

"Christian, I was bored at school today. It's so much more fun working at the store with you than going to class," she proclaimed, her mouth full of bread and cheese.

"Addie, you need to complete your education so that maybe one day you can become a teacher or pursue another profession that you will enjoy," Christian explained.

"Well, if I want to be anything at all, I want to be just like Mother!" was Addie's quick—and genuine—response.

Addie knew her mother was happy being busy with her "work." Clara's latest project—bringing tourism to the island—was both exciting and creative. Clara and Will were extremely pleased with the success of the tourism campaign. Now, newspaper writers were visiting Prince Edward Island to learn more about the inns, food, culture, and natural beauty of the destination.

Clara helped schedule the reporters' visits, coordinating with local inns and taverns to host and feed them. She, Will, or one of the now-almost-grown Warren children would pick up the reporters at the dock or train station. Each prepared a rendition of the island's attributes, including its history and various offerings. They were all excellent representatives, and the tourism collaborative often requested "a Warren" to serve as the official greeter for these American guests.

These were exciting and enjoyable times for the family as they worked together to support their homeland and took pride in their accomplishments. The family was also becoming quite well known by the local government, which recognized and applauded their efforts. Their days were full and busy, and the family was thriving.

Saint Martha looked down at the sweet scene from above. Clara and Will had raised a loving, kind family that was close to each other and committed to helping others. It was a beautiful scene.

She wished with all her heart that she could make time stand still for this family, but unfortunately, she could not.

CHAPTER 6

Heartbreak

T ime passed quickly for the family, and with everyone so busy, it was easy for Will to conceal a small concern he had been carrying for some time. Now in his later forties, Will was the picture of health—tall, strong, and vibrant, seemingly ageless in many ways. Clara depended on him completely, as did all the Warren children, as well as the extended family.

But Will was keeping a secret he was reluctant to share. Each morning, when the sun rose, Clara bounded out of bed with her usual determined energy. Will was accustomed to joining her for an early breakfast before starting his workday, which was often very physical in nature.

Over several months, however, Will noticed that he felt exhausted upon waking—even after a long and restful sleep. His energy during the day diminished, though he did not let anyone know that he felt tired or even depleted after unpacking a large inventory addition for the shop.

Will had begun allowing his sons—particularly Christian and Bill, who were already fully grown—to take on more of the heavy lifting and physical aspects of daily work. No one questioned it; they simply assumed that their father was assigning them a larger role in the dynamic and fast-paced family business.

The stairs were becoming a new dilemma for Will. In the past, he could bound up a flight or two within seconds, hardly needing a moment to catch his breath. Now, however, he would look straight at a set of stairs and feel his heart race—could he make it up without stopping midway to catch his breath? Would Clara or any of the children notice how winded he was after climbing? What was happening to his body? Will felt as though it was betraying him, yet he kept silent about his concerns.

On a cold December morning, Will finally had to tell Clara the truth. The sun rose much later now, although Clara still rose by 6:00 a.m., before heading downstairs to start breakfast for the family.

This morning, Will slept past nine—an unusual occurrence for him. The children had all left for school and work, and Clara was in the kitchen, feeling anxious about Will. She had already checked on him once that morning, and he was sleeping so deeply that he did not even notice her in the room.

She went upstairs to discover exactly what was happening. This time, Clara was not quiet as she opened the bedroom door. She walked to the windows and pulled back the curtains, allowing the winter sunlight to flood the room. Making quite a bit of noise as she moved around the bed, Clara was surprised that Will did not stir.

She began to worry that he was not breathing, although she thought she could see the rise and fall of his chest beneath the covers. Growing a bit panicked, she pulled the covers down slightly. Finally, Will stirred. His face looked so drawn, and his complexion was nearly ashen.

Will slowly opened his eyes. How had she not noticed the dark circles beneath them? It seemed he was battling within himself to wake up, to understand where he was and what was happening around him.

"Will, are you unwell? I am sick with worry about you!" Clara exclaimed.

In a whisper, and with a slow tone, Will replied, "Clara, yes, of course I am fine. I'm just a little tired this morning."

Clara had endured too much in her life to believe him. She could sense when something was wrong, and she scolded herself for not recognizing it sooner.

"Will, it's almost ten in the morning now, and you've been asleep since nine last evening. I am very concerned about you."

Will cautiously pulled himself up from the bed. He felt weak and unsteady but was determined not to cause Clara any more distress.

"Let's see if we can get you downstairs for some coffee and breakfast. A little nourishment might help," Clara said as she watched him get out of bed and get dressed. She had no idea how nervous he was about going down the stairs to the kitchen, and he quickly assured her that he would meet her there momentarily.

After washing up—splashing cold water on his face to fully awaken—he carefully descended the stairs. Clara had a steaming cup of coffee and a hearty breakfast plate prepared for him. Will sat down and began sipping the brew.

"There, Clara, I'm doing just fine. I just needed a good rest and a strong cup of your coffee to revive my weary soul," he said with a forced chuckle.

Clara did not believe him for a second. Now she was beginning to grasp the entirety of what was going on. She had been so occupied with the children, her work on the tourism board, and the store donation program that she had overlooked what was happening right in front of her.

"Will, I have seen when someone's health declines. I have witnessed too many people I love succumb to deteriorating health. I have no intention of helplessly allowing the same to happen to you." Clara was loving yet firm in her tone. "It's time you see a doctor; I'll arrange a visit immediately."

Will was too tired to argue.

Dr. Reilly was a fine man who often visited the Warren family when anyone had an ailment. That day, he came to see Will before any of the children had arrived back home. After an examination and a difficult quest for honest answers from Will about how he had been feeling, the doctor came to his conclusion.

"Will, you know your mother died from heart failure, don't you?"

Will simply nodded in agreement. Of course, he was aware of this harsh reality, but he had always believed he inherited his father's strong constitution.

"Well, it seems you might have the same condition. You are still vibrant in many aspects and are generally in good health, but your heart isn't as strong as it should be, and you will need to make adjustments for it going forward in your life."

"And what exactly do you mean by that?" Will demanded of the doctor, unaware that Clara was standing in the doorway, listening to their conversation.

"I know how hard you work in the store, Will. We all see you and your family bringing in the many items from the ships. Although you may want to continue doing this type of hard, physical labor, your body cannot—and should not—do it. You would be at risk for a full heart seizure if you don't slow down."

The remedy was clear: a less active life. Will was infuriated and in denial, but Clara quickly intervened.

"Doctor, won't walking on the beach with me or the children be good for his health? We can certainly handle the heavy lifting since we have three strong sons, along with his brothers and nephews for assistance. Let's focus on the things Will can do and move toward the future."

"This is not a death sentence unless you make it one by pushing yourself too hard," Dr. Reilly stated decisively. "Heart failure does not get better; it can only worsen. Our goal is to keep you safe by limiting excessive physical activity. I know it's not what you want to hear, but it's important to heed my words and take care of yourself. Clara and the children need you."

Will begrudgingly agreed. That night, at dinner, the family discussed the diagnosis and how everyone could help. Will and Clara committed to a daily walk along the beach—good for the body and soul, she said—as well as a way for Will to be at the store but not as physically active. He would supervise the comings and goings, and everyone would chip in on the "heavy lifting" needed.

Clara went straight to her desk after Will's health scare and retrieved the novena. This time, her prayer was specific: to keep Will alive and with her family for as long as possible.

Clara recognized how fortunate they were to have discovered his heart condition and to be aware of it. The older boys were eager to take on the extra responsibility, and the family once again came together as a united front.

Had Saint Martha heard her pleas? Perhaps she did, as Will was still alive, thankfully.

Although Will was unhappy with his diagnosis, he appreciated Clara's determination to refuse to let it change their lives. Their daily walks were cathartic and brought them even closer together. Time went by quickly and uneventfully while Will complied with his new reality.

Christian was now twenty-four and thriving at running the store. Bill, just two years younger, also yearned for more responsibility within the business. Some of the cousins were assisting with procurement, and they were increasingly trading with the American states instead of making the long journey across the sea.

Bill requested that he travel for business, and his request was approved. Will felt proud of his son for demonstrating such initiative. The entire family was eager to contribute so that Will could manage the business without the physical demands it entailed.

Clara and Will had learned to navigate the challenges of his illness. Although his heart condition posed some difficulties, Will never conveyed his disappointment about his health; instead, he focused on the positive and embraced each day. He enjoyed watching his children gradually take on business responsibilities and took great pleasure in Clara's ongoing dedication to her activities.

They had been dealt a blow, but they had survived it, at least for now.

The day the Warren family's world truly changed forever felt like any other day. It was September, a warmer-than-usual weekday beneath the bluest of skies. Each member of the Warren family was busy with their respective tasks, with Addie just starting a new school year filled with excitement. Clara was preparing for a three-day, two-night tour with a reporter from Boston, crafting a wonderful island itinerary for him. Will was supervising the boys who were unpacking a shipload of new items for the store that afternoon, while the two older girls were heading to play practice after school.

Addie came home as usual and went straight to the store. Today was hectic there, with her father and all her brothers working to bring in some large items for display. It was a hot day—more like July than September—and the waters were still warm from the summer sun.

"Christian, there are so many helpers at the store today. Could you please take me to the beach for a swim? I am so hot and want you to have one last summer swim. It would be so fun for us to go. Please take me!" Addie relentlessly begged her older brother.

With his fair complexion, Christian was not much of a beachgoer or swimmer. While his brothers, most particularly Bill, were lovers of the sea, Christian always preferred working in the store and occasionally carving wood. But today, he did not seem to have a vital role at the store, so he gave in and agreed.

The coastline of Prince Edward Island is deeply indented with tidal inlets, sand dune formations, and steep bluffs that rise high above the sandy beaches. Christian did not mention to his father he was taking Addie to the beach. Everyone was so busy that they always assumed he would watch her each afternoon. So off they went. She prepared to swim, while he assumed he would sit by the shore to watch her.

Ever careful, Christian knew he would only allow Addie to go waist-deep at best to cool off. The sea frightened him. He hadn't inherited his family's love for the ocean—he hated to admit it, but it almost terrified him. Still, he was Addie's oldest brother and most trusted caregiver when their parents were unavailable.

The details of that afternoon remain unclear. Although it was a beautiful day, the tide was high and rough, with particularly large and relentless waves.

"Addie, just up to your knees, please," Christian insisted. "It's not a calm day out there, and I don't want you getting caught in a rip current."

Christian had only heard his parents shout these words to the other children when he was growing up, as he rarely went in the water.

"Oh, Christian, I'm just fine! The water is so warm, and I'm very hot! This is fun. Come on in with me."

"I'll keep an eye on you from here, but please do not go out any farther."

Addie was jumping up and down in the water with a joyful smile, throwing water from the sea straight into the sky with her arms. She was looking straight up into the sun when a wave hit her from behind and she lost her balance.

She fell face down into the water, and Christian panicked. He ran out to her but could not find her. A strong current pushed against his legs as he waded farther into the sea to search for his sister. Another wave crashed upon him, forcing him down, his mouth wide open and taking in water. Unsteady and flailing, he desperately tried to locate Addie. His heart pounded; his vision blurred by the raging waters. Yet he pushed onward, valiantly confronting the punishing waves that crushed him down like columns of steel.

And then, out of the abyss of raging water, as he gasped for breath, calling out for Addie with every last ounce of his strength, a massive wave engulfed him. Christian went down hard, hitting his head against the sand and rock beneath him. The fight had ended, and he no longer struggled; the battle with the sea was finally over.

A bright, shining light surrounded him, and a sense of peace and calm engulfed him. At that moment, he was no longer worried about Addie; he was not afraid. He felt love all around him. Squinting into the effervescent, glowing light, he saw a figure walk toward him.

It was a man, younger than his father, Will, who appeared slim yet strong. Christian gazed up at the man, who was smiling at him and bore an uncanny resemblance to him.

"Welcome home, Son," Arthur said, wrapping his arms around Christian and gently carrying him toward the light.

Addie felt cold when she woke up on the hard-packed sand, with seaweed in her hair and the taste of salt water in her mouth. A group of very concerned-looking adults were gathered around her. What was going on?

Apparently, two young men ran into the water and pulled her from the current's grip; one firmly patted her on the back until she coughed up water after they carried her from the sea to the beach.

"Where's my brother Christian?" she screamed, the first words that came out of her mouth. The men stared out at the sea but saw no one. *Where had Christian gone?*

Within an hour, the entire Warren family had been notified, and search parties were sent out in small boats combing the sea for Christian. It took four hours before they found his body, a mile from where the siblings had gone swimming.

Neighbors say that you could hear Clara's gut-wrenching cries of despair all night and throughout the following day. There was no consoling a mother who had just lost her firstborn.

Clara and Will aged overnight. Losing Christian was the hardest experience of Clara's life—worse than losing her parents, her beloved Arthur, or her homeland. It was worse than the fear of Will having a life-threatening heart condition. Christian was Clara's connection to the past and her life before Will in England.

Will, also in deep despair, knew that Clara's grief was overwhelming, and he feared losing her as well. The other children were all in shock. None could comprehend how such a beautiful day had turned into the worst day of their lives.

Bill immediately threw himself into the role of the now eldest, returning to take over the store, help his parents with all aspects of home life, and guide his siblings through this tremendous loss.

After Christian's death, Grandpa George was filled with deep grief. Bill immediately volunteered to move into Christian's room—a truly difficult task indeed—to assist his grandfather... as they all sought to come to terms with their sorrow.

Addie, once a child full of light and laughter, quickly became a shadow of her former self. She was quiet and contemplative, seldom speaking unless spoken to, and laughter had vanished from her soul. Grandpa couldn't even bring a smile to her face with his stories. He, too, had become a melancholy version of himself, seemingly overnight.

The healing would take years, and the family gathered as best they could to mourn the loss of a child like no other in the Warren family.

After a few months' time, Will called a morning meeting with Clara and all the children.

"My dear family, I know we are all devastated by the loss of Christian, our shining light. But it is time for us to go on living; it is what your brother would have wanted. He would wish for each of you to live your lives fully and remember him fondly, not with such sadness. This is a difficult task, but it is one we all owe to Christian as we move forward."

"But how, Father? How can we do this?" asked John, now twenty. "How can I be jolly with my friends when all I can do is think about my brother's tragic death?"

"John, each of us experiences life and death in our own time. Your brother was taken from us too young, but he is at peace now and would encourage all of us to return to living fully. Staying in endless sorrow isn't the solution. Honoring Christian is a far better way to pay tribute to him."

"Is there something we can do, then, that would honor him, Father?" Emma asked meekly.

"Yes, I believe there is—or there could be—if we unite to create a special tribute to Christian that we can all take part in, now and forever."

With that, Clara, who had been quietly sitting next to Addie, stroking her hair as both listened tearfully to the exchange, knew what to do.

"Will, let us all think about what Christian would have most wanted us to do to honor his life. This evening at dinner, we can all bring out ideas together and remember our beloved son and brother more thoughtfully."

Clara walked to her desk, with Addie following closely behind. "Mother, can I write at the desk with you and think of Christian and something special to do for him?" Clara nodded in agreement, and the two got to work, each recording their favorite remembrances of Christian. The desk guided them, making their journaling easier, lighter, and more comforting.

At dinner that night, there was the first lively conversation about Christian that the family had been able to have since his death. They discussed what he liked, funny stories of escapades he had experienced, thoughts on what his future might have been, and how to honor who he was. Clara had written a beautiful tribute to her boy, one that captured his life and legacy.

"Christian, our beloved firstborn son. The joy of having you in our lives can never be taken from us. Your kindness, compassion, and responsible nature helped each one of us during your all-too-brief lifetime. We mourn the loss of you here with us today and the potential of what might have been. However, we cannot remain in our unbearable sadness; it is time to honor you and let the world know about you. My heartfelt desire is to name our charity work after you and build upon it. I would like to propose we create The Christian Arthur Warren Caring House, a small home where those less fortunate can come and select goods and items that we can donate to improve their lives."

Addie smiled for the first time since the accident. "Christian would have loved that, Mother. While those thoughts came to you at the desk, I, too, had a vision for my brother."

She displayed a drawing of a small house with Christian's name at the top, featuring a charming sign that read, "All Are Welcome Here."

Over the years, Christian's Caring House, as it was most often called, welcomed newcomers to the island and those in need, providing much-needed home supplies. The entire Warren family volunteered at the House, and all felt Christian's presence during their work there.

As each Warren child reached adulthood and married, they continued to honor Christian through their work at the House. Clara and Will often thought about how happy their son must be to know that his spirit was helping so many.

The years went by swiftly, and during the next decade, Will and Clara celebrated the marriages of the four older Warren siblings. Will's father felt the absence of his grandson acutely, and the years following Christian's tragic death saw a significant decline in George's health—and his will to live. Grandpa passed away just two years after Christian, deepening the family's sadness.

Residents of Prince Edward Island came from all over the small island to bid George Warren farewell at his funeral; his reputation as a fair businessman and a caring community member had earned him deep respect from the locals. Will felt proud to hear the many tributes paid to his beloved father by dear friends and strangers alike.

Now firmly established in his role as Will's eldest son, Bill had done everything he could to support both his grandfather and father with the store. After his grandfather's passing and with Will's declining health, Bill and his wife began to take on more and more of the responsibilities for the Christian Caring House as well.

Will had slowed down considerably and was having trouble with many physical tasks. The stairs now often seemed insurmountable, so they made a first-floor bedroom out of their home's living room to avoid the stress to Will's heart.

Clara thanked Martha every day for the extra years with Will, yet she could not comprehend how Christian had been taken from her. Life's heartbreak seemed never-ending. And still, life went on . . .

John, Emma, and Louise were all busy now with work in the store and the charity, and were all married. With Addie's age gap from the other siblings, there was still one more Warren to move into adulthood.

Since Christian's death, although she was pleased with the charitable house named after her brother, Addie had never truly been the same since that tragic day at the shore. She found some contentment at school and formed friendships with the local girls, but her favorite activities still centered around home, her mother, and time at the desk.

One day, while her parents were at Christian's Caring House, Addie began examining the desk closely. It had numerous nooks and seemingly hidden compartments, all beautifully carved and perfect for storing letters and notes. She began to mindlessly rummage through a drawer she had never really opened before, since she rarely used the desk without her mother present.

As she carefully pulled the small drawer open, she noticed some very old, yellowing papers beneath more recent correspondence. Her curiosity was overwhelming, and she stealthily took out a frail envelope dated before her parents were even married.

She opened the letter. It was addressed to Clara from a man named Arthur Christianson, who appeared to be writing from a war in England to her mother. He signed it, "Your Loving Husband."

Addie pondered the significance of the letter. Christian's middle name was Arthur, and this man's last name was Christianson. As the eldest Warren boy, why hadn't Christian been named after her father, William? Why was Bill, the second son, named after him? Thoughts raced through Addie's mind. What other secrets did the desk conceal?

Addie was now a young woman, living with her parents and working alongside them. Will and Clara were "getting along in years," and as the only unmarried Warren, Addie sometimes felt a bit guilty that they still had to worry about her.

But Addie was happy with her life on the island, as well as her work in the family business and charity. Her days were fulfilling, and overall, she felt a contentment that only came from years spent thinking about her brother and the dreadful day of his death. Initially, she had blamed herself entirely for his passing, but as time went on, she recognized that she had been just a child, and that Christian's death was a tragedy—one that had shaken the core of her family but had not shattered them.

The family had spent ten years healing from Christian's death. Had Addie just discovered a secret in the desk that could hurt them all even more than that? She pondered it deeply and carefully returned the letter to its hidden spot in the desk. Resting her head on the smooth wood, she asked for answers, feeling an emotional exhaustion wash over her. If she could just lie here for a moment, she would know what to do.

Had she dozed, or was she awake and daydreaming? Addie did not know, but the voice that came to her was loving and kind.

"Addie, you have a beautiful family that loves you, and I know you love them too. Your mother and father are kind and caring, and they share a wonderful life together. The desk has its own history, just like each of us. In life, there are reasons for some secrets, and it is only the keeper who can decide if they should be shared," Saint Martha gently told her.

Immediately alert, Addie reached into the desk to read the letter once more. Did she really daydream the soothing voice that had come to her? Perhaps she was simply imagining things and had misunderstood the words in the letter.

She quickly rummaged through the desk's compartments to reread the letter but could not find it. Her heart was racing, and her palms sweated. The decades-old note had mysteriously disappeared.

She moved all the papers in her way—where could it have gone? Wait . . . underneath all her mother's documents, she found another piece of worn paper folded into a small square.

Addie gently unfolded the paper to avoid tearing it. She smoothed the delicate sheet open and was confused to find something she didn't fully understand. There, in her mother's handwriting, was a novena to Saint Martha.

CHAPTER 7

Adaptation

The novena was a surprise to Addie not only because it seemed to arrive out of nowhere—in the very corner where she had just made a major discovery in the desk—but also because her mother had never mentioned doing this ritualistic prayer before. The novena appeared very old and was dedicated to Saint Martha, a saint about whom Addie knew little, but she was determined to learn more.

Addie wrote the novena on a separate piece of paper, folded the original back into its tight square, and placed it in the same spot she had just found it. Then, she closed the desk and headed straight to the local Catholic church.

"Jesus had a special relationship with Martha, her sister Mary, and her brother Lazarus," the priest explained after Addie tracked him down and pleaded for his insights about the novena. Addie then discovered that Jesus was often a guest at Martha's home in a small village near Jerusalem. There, Martha took on the role of hostess—cooking and cleaning for her guests, often too preoccupied with her tasks to pay attention to the conversations around

111

her. At one point, Jesus reminded Martha that listening to him and her guests, as her sister Mary did, was what truly mattered—more than simply worrying about what food to serve them.

"We celebrate Martha as the patron of servants and cooks," he concluded. Addie thanked the priest warmly for his time and insight before dashing back home.

"Patron of servants and cooks." She pondered the statement repeatedly in her mind. Her mother had owned an inn in England, cooking and cleaning for many guests. Perhaps that was why this novena was so significant to her.

Regardless, Addie had discovered one more mystery about her mother—one more mystery that she was determined not to address with Clara.

It was Addie's birthday, and her family had organized a wonderful celebration for her. Since finishing school, Addie had taken on a significant role at Christian's Caring House but was eager to do more in terms of work. She had met many reporters who came to visit and write about tourism and had decided that she wanted to learn more about being a writer. Her many years of journaling with her mother at the desk had nurtured a love for prose.

"Father, I've thought of a way to help more people learn about the Caring House on the island. I plan to ask the editor of the *Sentinel* if I could pen a piece about the house," Addie announced one morning while the family was at the store sorting through donation items. It wasn't a request; it was a firm statement directed at the family.

Will, sitting in a chair and "supervising" the store's activities, smiled. He considered himself a lucky man—fortunate to be here today, watching this beautiful family in action as they swarmed about him like bees to honey. He may not have had the energy to fully participate in all the work, but his heart and soul were with them as they worked together seamlessly.

"Addie, that's a wonderful idea that combines two of your best skills—caring for others and writing!" Clara beamed.

"Yes, that's an excellent idea, Addie, and a new challenge for you to embrace as well," Will chimed in. They both felt that a new endeavor was essential to keeping their youngest child fulfilled.

Addie wrote an extensive article about the Christian Arthur Warren Caring House and her family's dedication to assisting islanders. She interviewed numerous recipients of items from the charity, whose stories were just as intriguing—if not more so—than the main focus of the piece.

Each story showcased grit and determination, reflecting the journey of moving to the island and making a home, leaving the past behind, and shaping a new future. Addie soon recognized that the profiles of the new islanders offered a glimpse into the evolving Prince Edward Island and might be suitable as a regular column in the paper. She decided to present a few stories to the editor for his consideration.

"The story of the Charity House is very nice, but I believe it could be refined to function more as an announcement," Editor McIntyre asserted. "However, these profiles of our new neighbors are both intriguing and thought-provoking. Why don't you bring me one each week? In fact, I recently met a young man and his family who moved here from Quebec—James Ryan, along with his mother and father. Let's find out more about those who have chosen to make this their home."

With that, he stood up from his desk and escorted Addie to the door. Now, all she had to do was find James Ryan from Quebec and convince his family to be the subject of one of her new newspaper columns.

Edward James Ryan was born in Quebec City, in the province of Quebec. Named after his father, the family called him by his middle name to distinguish the two. His mother, Eloise, was of English descent and raised in the Anglican Church, while his father was purely Irish—and an Irish Catholic at that. His mother was quiet and reserved, whereas his father embodied a rugged, untamed quality that felt raw and unrefined. However, when he was "in his cups," he exhibited an easy confidence. His manners were decidedly informal, even somewhat coarse— which often left his wife feeling vaguely humiliated.

The Ryan children were raised in their father's faith, which oddly mirrored the decision that Addie's own parents made for their family. Mr. Ryan was a strict Catholic and made it a point to let anyone who met him know where he stood regarding his faith.

James, the oldest of their four children, was deeply committed to caring for his parents, stemming from a latent anxiety regarding his father's treatment of his mother, Eloise. The other three Ryan siblings, now grown and working, had opted to remain in Quebec and were less enthusiastic about the quieter lifestyle that Prince Edward Island offered.

James's father walked with a limp and needed to retire early for "health reasons," as he put it, though all who knew him sensed that his health decline stemmed more from his drinking than from his physical ailments. His wife, ever obedient and demure, followed where Ed Ryan led. Eloise was a devoted mother and a loyal wife, and if she harbored her own thoughts about the move to Prince Edward Island, they remained her secrets.

On this glorious fall day, Addie found James down by the docks, inquiring about work. His parents had used their savings to purchase a small but comfortable cottage just outside the township and a stone's throw from the sea. James had been furiously working to get them settled into the two-bedroom home, but now he knew it was time he found employment to help contribute and to begin his new life here on the island.

"Well, hello there, James Ryan," Addie called out from across the dock. James, completely taken aback that anyone would know his name, looked up with a surprised expression on his face.

"Good day, miss," he replied politely. "How can I assist you today? And how did you know my name when I have only just arrived on the island?"

"I'm Addie Warren, and I work for the newspaper, Mr. Ryan. My editor knows all the comings and goings here on Prince Edward's. We are doing a series of profiles on families relocating from other provinces and would love to talk to you about how you chose to settle here."

James chuckled. "It wasn't exactly my idea to leave the excitement of Quebec City for a tourist destination, but it was my parents' dream, so now it's my reality. But I'm not sure how compelling those facts would be for a newspaper article!"

Addie paused to consider his response. Would this truly make a good story? Her "journalistic" instincts swiftly concluded that it would.

"I believe this will indeed create a compelling story, especially about how their son devoted his future to making his parents' dream a reality. Would it be possible for me to schedule a time to visit your home and meet with you and your parents to gain further insight?"

"I'll check to see if they would like a visit from the local reporter. Why don't you plan to stop by later this afternoon after I speak with them? If they agree, we can chat about our journey here."

Addie asked for James's address. "Until we meet again," she exclaimed with a smile as she left the docks.

Addie was fully immersed in reporter mode as she quizzed James and his parents later that afternoon in their new home. James was twenty-three years old, the oldest of four siblings, each born just a year apart. He was a lanky young man with short, cropped light-brown hair and pale blue eyes. His complexion was fair, and his style leaned toward a more conservative, scholarly fashion that did not resemble that of the dockhands at all.

At his father's insistence, all four Ryan children attended Collège François-de-Laval in Quebec, due to its Catholic roots. His siblings, now twenty-two, twenty-one, and twenty years old, loved their lives in Quebec and outright refused their parents' request to move away. With a plentiful number of aunts, uncles, and cousins nearby—along with their strong loyalty to one another—the other Ryan siblings moved into an apartment close to their extended family, promising their parents that they would visit them and James often on Prince Edward Island.

"What type of work are you looking for here on Prince Edward Island?" Addie asked as she furiously jotted down his responses to her many questions for the article.

"Well, I would basically do anything—farming, helping at the docks, or working in one of the new inns—I'm happy to assist in any capacity needed."

Addie could not help but laugh to herself; this polite and incredibly handsome young man would undoubtedly fit in here on the island—but in her opinion, he would be better suited for an office rather than as a shipmate.

After completing the column, Addie titled the Ryan family profile "City Dwellers Seek Island Peace & Solitude," highlighting how the parents and their son transitioned from the hectic life of Quebec City to the tranquil, refreshing lifestyle of the island, characterized by its crisp sea breezes and breathtaking natural beauty.

The article featured a picture of the three Ryans standing in front of their new home. It mentioned James's quest for employment, and shortly thereafter, Clara returned from the tourism office with an exciting announcement.

"Addie, you know that new family you recently profiled in the paper? The head of the Tourism Department is looking for a full-time financial assistant and wants to interview the nice young man you spoke with. Do you happen to know how to contact him?"

Will looked up from reading the newspaper, and Addie nearly dropped the flower vase she was carrying to refresh its water in the kitchen.

"You mean James Ryan?" she said. Clara spotted a slight blush on Addie's cheeks.

"Yes, have you spoken to him lately?"

Addie felt somewhat embarrassed. She had certainly enjoyed meeting James and his family. She thought she might see him again, but three weeks passed, and she had neither run into him nor heard from him. She gave Clara the contact information and wondered how the Ryan family was faring.

The tourism executive director interviewed James the following week. James's affable personality and extensive background in finance proved a good fit, leading to his hiring at the agency.

Feeling more settled and confidently employed, James visited the newspaper one afternoon. He was fascinated by Addie; the spitfire reporter he had met a few weeks earlier. For weeks, he had hoped to bump into her around town, but this vague plan proved unproductive. Finally, one day, he decided to express his gratitude to the young reporter who had assisted him in finding work.

"Hello, Miss Warren," James said as he bounced through the newsroom. "Thought I would stop by and thank the inquisitive news reporter who helped me find a job here on the island."

Addie noticed that James was now wearing more traditional "island attire" and had abandoned his former stuffy style. He looked exceptionally handsome in his narrow, tailored pants and vest, having left his jacket back at the office before taking a quick stroll to the newsroom from the tourism offices.

Addie smiled. She had been quite taken with this fine young gentleman during their interview, and now she was equally pleased that he appreciated her work as a reporter.

"May I invite you to lunch this week?" James asked politely.

Addie felt that familiar warmth rise to her cheeks. "I would like that very much," she replied. A plan was made, marking the beginning of Addie and James as a couple.

After a few lunches together, Addie felt it was time for James to meet her family. She hadn't spent any time with James's parents since the initial day of the interview with them, but Addie was so close to her parents that she simply could not wait for them to meet this special man in her life.

For reasons she could not fully understand, James reminded Addie of Christian. He bore a slight resemblance to her late brother in stature, but it was more James's values and family connections that revived a part of Christian for her.

On the evening James came for dinner at the Warren house, Clara was startled to meet him. Although she had seen his photo in the paper and knew he was working in the financial department of the tourism office, she had not yet met him in person. Clara was astonished when she came face-to-face with James. *How could it be that Clara's "baby girl" had found a man who evoked the essence of both Arthur and Christian?*

Will was delighted. "What a fine young gentleman you've found, Addie," Will said after James had left and the three were clearing the dinner dishes.

"I'll take a seat so I can talk without getting out of breath." Will did what he could to help and then excused himself to a chair in the kitchen to be near Clara and Addie as they cleaned up the remainder of the meal.

"I believe I may have found my future husband," Addie beamed. Clara and Will nodded in agreement, their hearts brimming with hope for their youngest child.

James and Addie were having a wonderful time in their new life together. Addie took James on several tours of the island, and they spent much of their time with the Warren clan, which allowed James to get to know Addie's many siblings, their spouses, and their children. He was also intrigued to learn more about the impetus behind the establishment of Caring House, along with the history of the family store.

However, Addie was wondering why James had not brought her back to visit with his parents since she had conducted the interview months earlier. While James was almost constantly with her family, they had spent virtually no time with his parents.

One day, she gently brought this to James's attention.

"James, don't you think it's time we had dinner with your family? Or at least visit with them now that we are courting? I feel as though they don't know me, and I'm eager for them to meet my family as well."

James was quiet and hesitant in his response.

"Addie, I haven't wanted to bring this up, but my father is against our courtship because you were raised as a Protestant and our family are very strict Catholics. He believes that a marriage could not be solid unless the children are raised in the Catholic faith, just as we were."

Addie stared at James in complete disbelief. Was he really suggesting that she needed to become Catholic and raise their children in his faith if they decided to marry? Her mother had opted to raise her children in a different faith than her own—but that had been Clara's choice, not Will's. For Addie, religion was a personal matter, and no one should claim that their religious identity was superior—or more important—than anyone else's.

"Addie, I'm confident that you are the woman I want to spend the rest of my life with, and I do not want you to feel that my father's opinions hold more weight than yours. If we choose to build a future together, we will address our family matters on our own. My father will have to either accept it or not."

Addie had a distinct feeling that this proclamation would be a lot harder than James was anticipating . . .

Ed Ryan had come to Quebec from Ireland. It was a bold move at the time and one that was uncommon, as the English and Scottish were the most prominent settlers in the provinces, with Quebec having a large French population as well. Ed came with two of his brothers, seeking work to send funds back to their large Irish clan. He did backbreaking labor, as did his brothers, and took whatever jobs they could find.

Their solace was weekly Mass at Saint Patrick's in Old Quebec City, where Irish immigrants in the city congregated. His brothers eventually found Irish Catholic women at church to marry, but Ed fell in love with Eloise, a quiet, sweet young woman from their neighborhood. He was already head over heels for her before he realized she was of a different faith. However, Eloise didn't mind going along with any of Ed's ideas; that was just the kind of woman she was. All she wanted was a husband and a family; she didn't need a fancy life. Ed fit the role perfectly.

Ed and Eloise led a modest existence in Quebec. In quick succession, they had four children, and Eloise found joy in being a mother who lovingly nurtured her brood. Ed worked hard, returning home from the various factories he rotated between, often tired and irritable. He toiled in lumber yards, paper mills, shipbuilding, and metal foundries—wherever they needed strong workers. The constant factor was the conditions: The work was grueling, dangerous, and poorly paid, which only contributed to Ed's downward spiral into alcoholism. James bore the brunt of his father's bad moods, and Eloise greatly appreciated how her eldest could soothe Ed—she didn't know what she would do without him.

However, Ed began to feel the effects of his labor due to worsening health. In his final stint working in a textile mill, he spent long hours in poorly ventilated factories, dealing with heavy machinery that caused numerous minor but painful injuries. The noise of weaving looms and spinning machines was deafening, and the air was thick with cotton or wool fibers, leading to respiratory issues.

Finally, he felt it was time to retire, wanting to be as far away from the city's noise as possible. As always, Eloise didn't question or try to intervene in Ed's planning. Although she would leave three of her adult children behind, she was fine with it—her place was with her husband, as long as James was there as a buffer.

James never truly felt he had a choice about moving with his parents. How could he possibly leave his mother alone with that curmudgeonly man? So off to Prince Edward Island he went, never imagining he would find love and a wonderful family, who welcomed him as one of their own.

As a strong-willed young woman from a loving and stable family, Addie was now confronted with the reality that she loved a man from a completely different background. James seemed loving and kind, but what if he inherited some of his father's traits? Addie determined it was time to learn more about James's family, and she was resolved to do just that.

Addie knew that James planned to ask her to marry him, and she was thrilled at the prospect. She had secretly learned from her sister Emma that he had already met with her father to seek her hand. So, at this point, the only question was when he would propose. However, Addie did not feel comfortable accepting until she had spent some time with her potential future in-laws.

"James, I insist we visit your parents this week. We have been together for almost a year now, and you have not brought me to your home even once since I first met them. This is not right or fair. They need to know me, and I need to understand them."

An uneasy silence fell. James did not know how to respond. He understood that his parents would likely be unaccepting and that his father might not be kind to Addie. It had been one thing to meet her when she was a reporter writing a story about them last year, but now she seemed like a threat—someone who could potentially take their son away from them.

"I'll arrange it," he finally said. "But I'm afraid that it will change how you feel about me once you learn more about them."

"It's impossible, James. I love you—every part of you. And I need to understand the people who brought you into this world and those you've supported throughout your life."

With that, it was decided: They would have supper at his parents' cottage on Friday.

Eloise Ryan was nervous. She was accustomed to cooking for Ed and James, but certainly not for her son's reporter-turned-love-interest. She wasn't particularly worried about impressing Addie with her culinary skills, knowing that Ed had plenty to discuss with both James and Addie during this meeting.

Perhaps she should have felt more excited about their relationship, as this was a young woman who had captured the affection of her beloved son. However, Eloise also realized that Ed was determined to put an end to this "interfaith" relationship—and if James decided to marry, who would take care of them? She prepared the house for their guest, placed a small chicken in the oven to roast alongside some potatoes, and settled into her favorite chair to wait for what was to come.

James went to Addie's house to escort her to his family dinner. As he left to get her, he heard his father talking to himself in his room, sounding like he was rehearsing a speech. James had a sense of what his father was likely preparing to say during this visit, and it made his throat tighten.

Confident in his love for Addie—and hers for him—he was taking this significant step before Addie agreed to marry him. Addie needed to understand the family he came from and to freely decide if she could be a part of it.

They arrived at the house at six o'clock sharp—Ed did not tolerate tardiness. Both parents stood at the door to greet the young couple. Eloise attempted to muster a hospitable tone and engage in small talk as they entered the living room. Ed grunted a "Nice to see you again, Miss Warren," as he followed them.

James led Addie to the sofa and sat down next to her, while his parents took their seats in the two armchairs across from them. Before anyone could engage in further conversation, Ed launched into a verbal onslaught.

"Addie, James mentioned that you have lived on the island your entire life and haven't traveled beyond this point. Do you have any knowledge of where we are from? Have you seen the City? Are you aware of the factories and trade there?"

Addie stammered that her family frequently traveled to procure goods for the store and that she had met many travelers during her years of working there, hearing a lot about Quebec City and other areas, even Boston to the south.

"You've heard 'stories' . . . I understand, but you really haven't gone very far, have you?"

What kind of welcome was this? Why was she being treated so poorly by the father of the man she loved?

"James mentioned that you weren't raised Catholic, even though your mother was brought up in the true Church. Why is that?"

James was getting exasperated—and they had only been at the house for a few minutes.

"Father, that is enough. Addie's family has made their own choices about worship, and Addie has decided on her own travels. I would appreciate it if you could stop this unpleasant inquisition."

Ed did not respond positively to his son's apparent role as Addie's protector. "Son, we do not approve of this relationship. So if you do not choose to end this imperfect match immediately, you will lose our support and must leave this house."

James stood up, gently took Addie's hand, and the two walked out the door.

Clara and Will felt devastated by the news of the meeting.

"James, I am so sorry that your father has placed you—and all of us—in such a difficult position. Being forced to choose between the family of your birth and the family of your future is unfair. Clara and I truly believe that there is always enough love to include both in one's life," Will said to the couple from his chair by the fireplace.

"Son, you can stay in our attic apartment while you and Addie decide your next steps. Please let us know how we can assist you."

Clara took James upstairs to help him get settled. In the morning, he would return to his parents' house to collect his belongings. He felt a mix of sadness and hope. He cherished the family that raised him, yet he adored the family that would become his as well, once he and Addie were married.

Addie felt emotionally drained from the events of the evening. She excused herself from her family and retreated to her favorite sanctuary—the desk. There, she journaled late into the night, desperately seeking guidance on how to navigate these challenging waters. She refused to lose James because of his parents, but she also didn't want James to lose his parents because of her.

Addie let out a long sigh as she felt the sturdy wood of the desk and asked for the strength they would need to be together while still respecting James's family. The desk creaked under the weight of her arms and her soul-searching—or at least, that's how Addie perceived it.

The answers are in the desk, a small voice inside Addie's mind whispered. Addie slowly caressed the desk, carefully opening its many small compartments while being mindful not to disturb her mother's private papers.

And there it was, yet another small, folded note tucked into a crack in the desk. Addie took great care in removing it. How many messages did this magical desk hold? What might this particular note possibly say—and who could it have come from?

Why had she only noticed it now?

She read the note aloud:

Love is God's greatest gift. It is worthy of being
fought for and should be cherished and honored.
Love will give you the strength you need to conquer
the battles ahead.

CHAPTER 8

Strength

Addie stared at the paper for a long time. She thought of James, how he made her laugh and feel lighter each time they were together. He was her support, her partner, her future. She wanted to marry James with all her heart. But how does one marry a man whose parents oppose the union? James had been so loyal and dedicated to his parents. Could he—would he—put her before them?

She started to cry, and her tears fell upon the secret note. Her heart was breaking. She felt short of breath, dizzy, sad, angry—a million emotions all rolled into one. Then, she looked down on the note again, trying to gain strength from its message.

Oh no! The letters were vanishing from her tears. All she could see now was a cryptic group of words, and those were also fading quickly—

Love
fought
cherished
strength
battles

She reached for something to write with and carefully jotted down the words she could remember as they faded into the tear-stained paper.

Addie wrote: *Cherish love and find the strength to fight for it.*

That had to be her message from the desk, as it was all she could feel at that moment.

After James settled into his room in the Warren attic, he asked to meet with Will.

"Sir, I don't know what the path forward will be, but as I said before, I would like to ask for Addie's hand in marriage. I promise to be a good, loving husband and put her before others, as I have witnessed you do with your wife. I sincerely hope you trust me to do so and will give us your support."

Will, weary from Addie's angst but fond of James, said, "James, you have my and Clara's support, and we are here for you and Addie as you navigate these difficult waters."

With that, James thanked Will and excused himself. It was time to visit with his parents and come to some type of solution.

As he walked to his parents' home, James's mind raced. He loved his parents, but he recognized that he had spent a lifetime caring for them, intervening when his father was verbally abusive and assisting his mother with tasks that his father could have and should have managed himself. James had prioritized his family over himself, sacrificing to move here with them when none of his siblings would agree to come.

Although his father was a difficult man, James felt compassion for him. As a child, he listened intently to his father's tales of an ill-fated life and the hard work he endured in filthy factories, moving from one to another as work dried up.

James always believed that his father was merely angry about the difficult work he had to undertake to support the family. However, he was unaware that Ed's suffering ran deeper than that.

In his own mind, Ed Ryan may have had a loving wife and four good children, but he could not move past the anger about his lot in life. He held higher visions and hopes for himself, but they never materialized. His brothers were softer than he; they merged into their wives' families, who helped them secure better jobs over time as they transitioned off the factory lines.

Ed's wife, Eloise, was profoundly disconnected socially and unable to support him. It was his own misfortune in life to have fallen in love with and married a girl from the wrong church without any family support. His children often felt like absolute burdens to him—four mouths to feed and bodies to clothe. Ed's resentment continued to simmer each year in the boiling pot of his mind.

James was calm as he approached his parents' home. Little did he know that his father had been stewing for days over his possible marriage to Addie. No son of his would ever walk away for a woman! What kind of boy had he raised? His anger boiled over and became directed at his wife, whom he blamed for this turn of events.

"You raised him to be so weak!" Ed roared at Eloise. "He doesn't listen at all—and has the audacity to choose what he calls 'love' over his obligation to his birth family. I am disgusted and will never call him my son again."

Eloise, frightened by her husband's anger yet sadly accustomed to it, did not respond. The tirades didn't always last long. He may have been cruel with his words, but thankfully, he was not violent—for that, Eloise was grateful. Men get angry; it's just the way they are made, she would tell herself. Let the storm pass by holding on and riding the waves. Somehow, she had managed to do this for decades.

James used the door knocker, which felt strange to him since, until recently, this had also been his home. His mother slowly opened the door. She was so happy to see James that she wanted to throw her arms around him but knew better than to do so. Without saying a word, she motioned for him to enter the house, where a red-faced Ed stood, sweaty and panting from walking in circles in the small living room.

"How dare you come here!" he faced James and screamed. "You are not welcome here. You are no longer my son! You can take your Protestant woman and go become a pagan like her and her mutt family. Your mother and I have no use for you anymore."

Indeed, Ed had already contacted James's younger brother Paul and told him James could no longer help them. Ed then lied to Paul, telling him that James was moving off Prince Edward Island with his soon-to-be wife.

"Your brother Paul is on his way. He will assist your mother and me here; your help is no longer needed."

"Why are you making Paul come? I am living right here on the island and will soon marry Addie. I will be right here to help in any way."

"I told your brother you and your new bride would be leaving soon for new ventures. Good luck with everything, James. I hope she's worth the price you are paying."

With that, Ed gestured toward the door. James cast a sorrowful glance at his mother, but she refused to meet his eyes. She was a woman who stood by her man, prioritizing her husband over herself and her children. And that is precisely what she did.

"I will visit again once Paul arrives."

"Do as you wish; Paul can visit you outside our home, but not within it. You are no longer welcome here."

James was deflated. He had always known how cruel his father could be. He had seen it in how he treated his mother, in how he talked about his fellow factory workers, and in his onslaught of derogatory language about other immigrants in Quebec. The man was full of hate, but somehow, James was not. James's temperament was unlike that of his father. He was his own man, and he would now fully start his own life with Addie.

That night, James took Addie for a long, moonlit walk. Arm in arm, they first strolled through the township and then down toward the shore, careful to avoid the area where James's family had settled. They walked along the beach—at the exact location of Christian's accident all those years ago. Addie felt Christian with her, giving her strength as well.

"Addie, you are the love of my life. Unfortunately, my family has forced me to choose—you or them. And I choose you, now and forever. I hope with all my heart that you will see me for who I truly am and not as an extension of my family. I promise to put you and our children before all others. Addie, will you please marry me?"

Addie leapt into his arms. "Of course I will marry you, James. My heart is heavy that you had to make this choice, and perhaps someday your parents will accept us together. We don't know what the future holds, but I am willing to fight for our love and cherish it now and forever."

The words from the note were emblazoned in her mind. This would be a love she had to fight for, and she would do so with all the strength she possessed.

Invitations to the wedding were sent out within the next few weeks. As James was living at the Warren home, the family hurried to find accommodations for the soon-to-be newlyweds. Through Will's many contacts on the island, they found a comfortable guesthouse available for rent from an older widow who was now living alone in a far-too-large home. Feeling a bit lonely and isolated, she gladly rented the carriage house to the young couple.

Arrangements for the wedding were made for the third Saturday of the month. The local reverend was delighted to accommodate Clara's request for a midmorning service, followed by a lovely luncheon at the social hall in the center of town. Emma and Louise would be the bridesmaids, while Bill and John would usher the guests into the church.

James hoped his two brothers would be groomsmen and that his sister could join Addie's wedding party. However, all the Ryan children were forbidden from attending. Bill and John quickly assured James they would stand by him at the altar.

The day was glorious. Addie was a vision in her tulle gown and long flowing veil. Rather than mimic the voluminous hairstyles of the day, Addie chose to wear her thick, long curly hair down, simply pulled back from her face with a soft satin bow at the back. Clara had remade Emma's wedding gown as well as the veil from Louise's wedding into a stunning ensemble that suited Addie perfectly. Addie was a breathtaking bride, her welcoming smile and twinkling eyes on full display as she began her procession down the aisle.

That day, Will felt particularly worn out, so it was decided that both he and Clara would escort Addie down the aisle to the altar. This break in tradition was necessary—each step was deliberate and exhausting for Will. As Clara and Will walked arm in arm with Addie on either side, Clara surveyed the scene around her.

James was smiling from ear to ear, his gaze fixed solely on Addie. Emma and Louise looked beautiful in their sage green dresses on one side of the reverend. On the other side, flanking James, were Bill and John, tall and handsome—the spitting images of their father, Will. They were bighearted, fine young men of whom Clara was so proud. The sun shone down the walkway, almost blinding the three of them as they made their way down the aisle.

As Clara looked up, she almost tripped on her dress seam. Was that another young man standing at the altar? Tall, blond, and thin in stature, he was smiling at Addie with an undeniable gaze of adoration.

No, her mind was playing tricks on her. Yet Clara felt his presence because there, at least in her mind, stood Christian—waiting for his beloved sister alongside his brothers. Will, who had been carefully looking down as he took each step, gazed up. He, too, saw the vision.

Addie was the last to raise her gaze. The sunlight streamed so brightly through the stained-glass window panels that she struggled to find her beloved groom, James. There he was—right in the center, with the most loving smile on his face. Indeed, on either side of James stood her two sisters and three brothers.

Yes, three brothers. And in that moment in time, the Warren family was united once more.

Clara and Will were delighted for Addie and James. The wedding was a wonderful day full of love and laughter. If James was saddened by his family's absence, he never showed it. He adored Addie and knew that his new life had just begun. Yet he had not given up on his family, either.

Although James's siblings did not attend his wedding due to his father's threats, he knew they would eventually come around. Paul was moving in that week, and soon, James could talk to him in person and end this nonsensical stalemate. Life was far too short for a feud over his marriage.

The years and his heart condition had taken a toll on Will. Although he remained as handsome as ever, he was thinner now. His appetite had diminished without his usual active days. He needed to nap each afternoon and slept for up to ten hours each night. Yet he was completely mentally alert and presided over the family and the business in a kind, loving, and always present manner. For that, Clara was forever grateful.

Clara seemed ageless. Her blonde hair beautifully blended with the new silver strands that came with her age. Her skin remained flawless, with only the wrinkles around her crystal blue eyes appearing as "smile lines," as Will called them. She was strong and vibrant, often mistaken for the older sister of her three daughters. Clara remained as active as ever, enjoying her role as a tourism volunteer and making visits to her youngest son-in-law at the office when she attended meetings.

Addie had continued her journalism career, now working as a features writer for the *Prince Edward Island Magazine*. Within a few short months after their wedding, Addie learned she was pregnant, and both she and James were thrilled. Unfortunately, he had not yet reconciled with his family and was determined to do so now that he was to become a father.

On a raw, rainy winter afternoon, James decided it was time to visit his parents once more. His attempts to date had been thwarted, and his parents had somehow turned his brother Paul against him. However, James resolved to mend the relationship between the Warrens and the Ryans.

As he approached the cottage, James could see his brother through the living room window. Paul looked thin and anxious. He was standing next to his mother as Ed walked in small circles in an animated manner, hands in the air as he spoke to them—a familiar scene for James. When James knocked on the door, Paul answered and looked relieved to see him.

"James, thank you for coming by. Please help me with Father; he is not well and is talking nonsense. Mother and I do not know what to do," Paul exclaimed. This sudden turn of events shocked James.

"Get him out of here," Ed slurred, his voice revealing that he had been drinking. "He's not my son, and if you let him in here, then you're not my son either."

Paul and James exchanged glances. They surveyed the room. Eloise was practically hiding behind a chair while Ed was stumbling and incoherent.

"Father, that's enough. Let's get you some coffee and sober you up," James calmly stated.

Ed was having none of it. He began pushing books off the shelves and then throwing china from the cabinet against the walls. For the first time in their lives, the brothers witnessed their father completely come undone.

Then, the unthinkable happened. After over thirty years of marriage to Eloise, without ever harming her—

even during his most horrible rants—he aimed a crystal vase at the boys. But just before he threw it, Eloise let out a piercing scream, "No, Edward!"

He turned and put all his rage into that vase and aimed it directly at her, hitting the side of her face and knocking her to the floor. Blood splattered from a jagged cut on her forehead as she slumped over. *What had he done?*

The police arrived within minutes. The neighbors, having heard the scream, alerted the authorities. As Eloise was taken to the local hospital, Ed Ryan was handcuffed and taken to the jailhouse. Paul and James went to be with their mother, disgusted and finished with their cruel, sick father.

Addie could not believe the series of events. Over the next few days, James and Paul planned for their father to be taken to the Prince Edward Island Hospital for the Insane instead of pressing charges against him. They sincerely hoped that receiving mental health care would be better than him spending a few years in jail.

Eloise had suffered a concussion and needed over thirty stitches on her forehead. The attending physician said that she would most likely have a scar for life where the vase crashed into her head. Eloise thought it was a small price to pay for finally doing something to defend her children from their abusive father. She felt a sense of pride in knowing that her scream had diverted Ed's attention to her, saving her boys from the monster she had married.

After a few days, it was decided that James and Addie would move into the Ryan cottage and that Paul would bring his mother back to Quebec, where she would live with their sister and her husband. James would visit his father weekly at the hospital here on the island and hope for the best in terms of his recovery. For now, Addie and James would pack up their belongings from the carriage house and bid farewell to their landlord.

"James, how are you feeling about all these terrible happenings?" Addie asked the night after his father's rage incident.

"I feel sad, profoundly sad, but also relieved. It was time for my father to end his reign of unbearable control over our family. I certainly wish it hadn't happened in this manner but now my mother and brother are safe, and my father is finally receiving the help he needs." Knowing that his father was now securely detained by the province at the institution brought a level of ease for all of them.

"I believe your mother will be happy again once she is settled with your sister. She loved Quebec and missed your sister and brothers. We will be sure to visit them in time, especially once we have the baby."

The two held each other closely. Life had not been easy for James Ryan. He did not grow up in a family like the Warrens. But now he was a part of them, and Addie was so relieved for him—and for herself, and their unborn child. It was time to begin their life together, free from the negativity and fear that had been such a part of James's entire upbringing.

Clara and Will were also shocked by the course of events. Although the circumstances were not ideal, the outcome was likely the best it could be. Will had been concerned about Ed Ryan and his influence over James. He feared it would become difficult for the couple to establish a relationship with James's parents, especially after the baby was born. Hopefully, the man would receive the help he needed, but for now, he was locked away and could not hurt Will's beloved daughter and her family.

Clara grappled with conflicting thoughts about what had transpired. James's father was an actual monster capable of trying to harm his own wife and children. He was mentally unstable, angry, and violent. She prayed that James had inherited none of Ed's demons and that he would always possess the strength to be his own person.

And she prayed that Addie would have the courage to fight for her, James, and their children. One day, Ed Ryan would be free again, and his anger could be directed toward them . . . but these were negative thoughts, and Addie and James needed support and love at this moment.

Clara approached the desk to write in her journal. Expressing her feelings on paper always brought her solace.

As she wrote, she noticed a crumpled paper that looked as though it had been thrown there. It was in the far corner of the room, diagonally opposite the desk. It was a ragged note with just a few words scrawled on it. Since only Clara and Addie ever sat at this desk, she realized it must have been Addie's writing.

All Clara could discern were a few words, yet the message was clear. Addie had already learned that she needed to fight for love and cherish it. Clara could not have imparted a better lesson to her.

With that, Clara closed her journal and left the desk to go to bed with the man she loved and cherished. Clara would fight for Will and her family until the day she died, and she knew that Addie was ready to do the same for her family.

Addie and James welcomed a baby girl that spring. They named her Rose, believing she was as stunning as a rose in bloom on a sunny day. Rose Marie Ryan was a sweet, happy baby, and Clara was thrilled to once again be "Grammy" to a newborn.

Addie, ever independent, continued writing for the magazine after the baby was born. Slightly ahead of her time, she was confident that women could work and parent simultaneously.

Clara chuckled at Addie's determination to take as little time off work as possible after giving birth. Of course, Addie's circumstances were not that difficult—little Rose had a host of aunts and uncles, as well as two grandparents who were all eager to assist.

The island's robust economic years were giving way to more difficult financial times. Although the store was still a stalwart part of the township economy, many other industries—most notably shipbuilding—were in severe decline. Many locals were looking for work, and the Charity House was busier than ever.

With Addie writing for the magazine so often, Emma and Louise had taken over much of Christian's Charity

House's day-to-day work. They were seeing an increasing number of their neighbors in need of donated goods.

Times were becoming increasingly difficult, prompting Louise to suggest that the family establish a food pantry for damaged canned and boxed goods that could not be sold in the store. The pantry would provide these items to those in need within the community. Will and Clara were pleased with the idea.

"We've fostered a spirit of giving in our children, Clara, and for that, I could not be prouder. I thank you for being my partner in this endeavor, which may be our family's greatest legacy," Will mentioned to Clara as he watched her sort burlap bags of beans for the food pantry.

"Will, we are fortunate to have more than enough. Prince Edward Island is our family home, and we must do what we can for our neighbors and friends in need."

As employment decreased in many industries, more families chose to leave the island and head for the "Boston States"—various towns and cities in the New England states of America.

Will had ventured to Boston, Massachusetts, many years earlier, but due to his health, he no longer traveled. Clara had not left the island since her arrival from England all those years ago. She was too content with her home life and had no interest in adventure after her long journey between continents.

Bill and John, along with their cousins, had made extensive business trips to Europe and the States. They raved about Boston, a fascinating city with a harbor on the Atlantic Ocean and robust international trade opportunities.

Clara's tourism commission had become worried about the island economy. The general population was diminishing rapidly as young families eager for better employment and to be part of the industrialized new cities were relocating in droves. Tourism was certainly down; James could attest to that as he researched each month's financial reports for the commission.

In September, following Rose's birth, James returned home from work with a worried expression on his face.

"Cheer up, James! It's a beautiful day, and your gorgeous daughter and wife both want a big kiss," Addie said as she looked up from her typewriter.

"Addie, we have to talk," James said solemnly. Addie was worried. Had his mother or father been in an accident or some other incident, and she had not heard? It was very unlike James to be so somber.

"The Tourism Department is eliminating my position at the end of this year. Our budget is significantly behind schedule, and they cannot support so many full-time staff."

Addie did not find the news that upsetting. Having been raised in a family of means, she did not understand that her husband's salary was extremely important to their lifestyle. Her parents had provided her and all her siblings with any financial help they needed.

"James, my parents will support us while you search for a new job. There's no need to worry at all. I'm confident that you'll find something you enjoy very soon."

"Addie, I don't think you fully understand. I know we are living in my parents' cottage, which has no payments, but I must send money to my mother each month, and I am responsible for covering part of my father's hospital care as well. After those two expenses—and with your salary—we have enough to live relatively comfortably. But there are not many jobs equivalent to the one I have now in the government. I fear I won't be able to make up the difference . . ." His voice trailed off.

"I'm considering exploring job opportunities in the Boston States," he went on. "I heard that work is abundant, especially for well-educated Canadians."

Addie stared at him in disbelief. Was he considering moving her and Rose to America?

The Winds of Change

Addie was incredulous; her mind raced. James must have been experiencing some sort of lapse in self-confidence. Of course he would find another position here on the island, and quickly at that. However, Addie knew, from the many neighbors now seeking assistance from the Caring House, that times were becoming tougher financially.

The magazine had shifted her role from full-time staff to assigning her stories only periodically; however, this arrangement suited Addie perfectly, as she was enjoying her time with Rose. In truth, Addie was unaware of the actual state of the island's economic depression.

Will, on the other hand, was fully aware of what was transpiring on the island. Sales at the store had decreased, prompting him to limit the travel that Bill and John were doing for procurement. He also cut expenses to ensure that all family members involved in the business could be adequately supported, and he was fortunate to have a substantial nest egg in the local Union Bank, which Will had switched to from the original Prince Edward Island Bank.

The Warren family had a long history on the island, and Will and his father were pleased to be early bank depositors. However, when Union Bank was formed, Will's many longtime commerce associates implored him to join its ranks. The bank's officers were mostly hardware and dry goods merchants, and Will felt that they better understood his business's needs. Many of the other banks were heavily involved in the shipbuilding industry, which was now experiencing a substantive decline.

"Clara, I know you understand the economic uncertainty of the times," Will began, sipping his cup of Clara's delicious morning brew, the aroma of which enticed him out of bed each day. "While we can support everyone in the family involved in the store, I recognize James's plight right now. He's his own man and wants to provide for his family."

Clara was in disbelief. Was Will really considering supporting James in his thoughts about moving to the Boston States? What on earth was he thinking? Clara could not even tolerate the prospect of Addie being so far away from her; and what about Rose and future children? Clara was firmly on Addie's side, believing that the young family should not move that far from their nuclear family.

"Clara, please remember that you moved far from your homeland with the man you loved. At times, one must take a leap of faith for their future."

"Will, I cannot imagine life without Addie here. I know she is a grown woman, but she will always be my baby. I love watching Rosie in the afternoons when Addie comes to write her articles for the magazine at the desk. And James fits so perfectly into our family. How could we possibly watch them leave?" Clara felt tears well up in her eyes, sensing this sad possibility.

"Why don't we simply watch and wait for now, my love? James has a few months to explore his opportunities here on the island. Perhaps something will arise for him."

Will returned to his coffee as Clara continued to silently worry about the future.

Just down the road, in the two-bedroom cottage they were "watching" for James's parents, another conversation was unfolding.

"James, I simply cannot—will not—leave my family. I have never even left this island! How could you even think of taking me and our daughter away from everything we love here?" Addie implored.

James had become quite enamored with the idea of a fresh start for his little family. He hated visiting his father weekly at the hospital. Although his father had become sober, he remained mean and cruel to James. Rather than embracing the help offered at the hospital, he picked on other patients and was combative with the nurses. Twice now, the head of the institute had threatened to send Ed Ryan to jail—his only alternative to his sentencing for the attack on James's mother.

The home where James and Addie lived was not theirs to keep; it belonged to his mother. His siblings were eager for James to sell the property to raise money for Eloise. As happy as she was with her daughter's family, it would be best for Eloise to have her own small living space nearby. The funds from the sale were needed for this transition, and the Ryan family was losing patience with James regarding the sale of the cottage.

James had been reticent to tell Addie about these developments in his family. She was so happy these days, engaging in all her passions, surrounded by her wonderful family, and cherishing their sweet little Rose. But times had changed, and they would soon need to adjust to new circumstances.

"Addie, I am doing my best to find another position here, but we are facing additional challenges. I need to sell the cottage soon to provide for my mother, and there is a high probability that my father will not be in the hospital much longer. His poor behavior toward the patients and staff is leading to a review next month—and the only alternative is the jail sentence we got him out of through the forced hospital stay."

"Well, we can just move in with my parents, James! They will love having us while we get back on our feet." With that, Addie left the room. She was certain that James would find a position soon, and then they could go back to see if that cute little carriage house they had rented before getting married was still available. However, it was quite small, and there was a distinct possibility that another baby was on the way—she had an inkling—but she hadn't wanted to tell James just yet . . .

James would miss his position in the Tourism Department, but he was not alone among those being asked to leave. The department would soon consist of a director and several volunteers, including a retired banker who would donate his time to handle the financial reports that James managed each month.

As he suspected, employment was scarce on the island, and he heard of more islanders leaving for better opportunities in the States. Without discussing the matter with anyone, James began sending job inquiries to financial institutions in the Boston area.

Many islanders settled in that area, all taking the Boston Boat from Prince Edward Island, a journey of just over a day. James hesitated to inform Addie about his prospecting there, so he pursued both quests simultaneously.

The happy news of Addie's second pregnancy soon spread through the family. Yet Addie foresaw that this next baby would not receive the same attention from the Warren family as Rose. Times seemed to be getting worse on the island, and Addie knew that James needed to make a move sooner rather than later.

As James had hoped, a few calls from Boston did come in—enough, in fact, for him to schedule a visit to the States in two weeks to meet with potential employers.

"James, I understand that you need to go to Boston to search for employment, but I am feeling very anxious about our future. I love being with my family so much; it feels overwhelming to me to move to a new country and start over," Addie pleaded.

James walked across the room and gently wrapped his arms around his beloved wife.

"Addie, if I didn't have to do this, I wouldn't. Unfortunately, we need to change course for our family to thrive. I know it's heartbreaking for you to think about leaving, but let me go explore Boston and see what I find. I won't make you do anything you believe you cannot. Even if I have to live in Boston and send money back to you and the children, I will, visiting when I can. But that is not how I hope we will live. Let's give this some time, and discuss it further when I return."

Perhaps James would despise this new city, Addie thought to herself. He had lived in one before, so he knew how busy a congested town with thousands of residents could be. She would put this out of her mind and concentrate on Rose, her articles, and her family. Her mother and father would certainly assist them if needed. For today, she would no longer think about a life off Prince Edward Island.

Over the following weeks, James made numerous inquiries to meet other Prince Edward Island "outmigrants"—Prince Edward Island natives who had moved to the States. He arranged a room at a boardinghouse where many newly transplanted islanders stayed in Boston and set up several meetings with former acquaintances of his and Addie's who now lived there with their young families. He even scheduled a visit to Dorchester—a Boston suburb where many immigrants lived—with an Episcopal Church reverend, in hopes that it might help Addie feel more comfortable with a move.

What James did not know was that Will was also working behind the scenes to help his son-in-law. Although Will was disappointed that James and Addie might need to leave the island, he was proud of James's initiative and pride. James wanted to make his own way for Addie and his children, and Will had great respect for that. James was independent and handled difficult situations beautifully. He would be a good steward for his growing family.

Once he knew James's Boston travel schedule, Will went to his bank and met with the president.

"Sam, my son-in-law James Ryan is going to Boston next week for meetings with potential employers. He is a fine financial professional, and his position was recently eliminated at the Tourism Department here on the island. I was wondering if you have any contacts at the banks in Boston who might need a dedicated worker with an excellent education and strong work ethic."

Samuel Eaton sat back behind his fine mahogany desk in his richly appointed office at the bank. Union Bank had merged over the years with the larger Bank of Novia Scotia, providing interactions beyond the island and into the States. Will Warren and his family were among his top customers—successful, loyal, and caring members of the community. Will had never asked Sam for a favor, and he was more than pleased to help, especially since the bank was doing more and more business outside the island.

"Will, give me a few days and let's see what I can do," Sam said, bidding Will farewell. Will understood that Sam would do everything in his power to help.

Within two days, Will met with James at the store and informed him about two opportunities in Boston that he hoped James would consider exploring during his visit the following week.

Both the Massachusetts Bank and the Suffolk Bank had several positions available; both were seeking clerks, a role for which James might be overqualified, but still a valid option. Meanwhile, the First National Bank of Boston was actively searching for an apprentice to begin as a clerk and progress into management. Graduates with higher education would be given careful consideration, especially those with a recommendation from Samuel Eaton, the president of the Prince Edward Island Bank of Nova Scotia.

James was ready to embark on the journey to America. Full of hope and trepidation, he prepared for his week-long visit to Boston.

Addie stood on the Charlottetown dock with Rose on her hip and tears in her eyes. It was Friday morning, and the Boston Boat was loading for its regular trip to and from Prince Edward Island to Boston Harbor. The seasonal steamer appeared enormous, and there was a flurry of activity as hundreds of passengers boarded—many with young children—seeking the prospect of a better life in the "Boston States."

The trip would take more than a day's time, stopping in Halifax before continuing to Boston. James would rest overnight in a berth, and meals would be provided on board.

James waved to Addie and Rose as he stepped onto the

vessel with his fellow travelers. He took comfort in knowing he would see some familiar faces in Boston and hear their stories of relocation to this new country. His hope outweighed his fear, and excitement grew within James as he boarded.

Addie could barely see through her tears. Born and raised on this beautiful island, she had no desire to venture to a new home beyond it. There was so much to see and explore here on Prince Edward Island; she loved every inch of its magnificent shoreline, rolling meadows, and the fresh sea breezes that filled the air.

Leaving felt unthinkable—an almost unbearable prospect. But James had visited every business on the island, and there were no job opportunities on the horizon. The store did not require any more help; Will could barely keep the staff busy enough these days.

So, with considerable hesitation, Addie agreed to support James in his quest, regardless of how much it broke her heart.

"Wave to your papa, Rose," Addie choked out to her smiling little girl, who was enchanted by the large ship and her father's thrilling journey.

"Bye-bye, Papa! Please bring me a toy back from Boston," the toddler hollered to her father.

"Will do, Rosie! See you in a week's time. Be a good girl for Momma, and I'll bring you back something special from Boston." With that, James was out of view and earshot, moving with the crowd onto the ship.

Addie and Rose walked the short distance from the docks back to Addie's parents' home. She knew that her father had assisted James with a few job opportunities there. Part of her felt grateful, while the other part was furious. Why did her father have to be an accomplice in this plot to take her away from her home?

Clara greeted Addie, her small baby bump barely visible beneath her dress. "Come in, my loves. I am sure you could use a cup of tea right now," Clara said as "the girls" arrived.

"Grammy, my papa is going to bring me a toy from Boston!"

"Oh, that is wonderful, Rosie! We will play with it once your father returns next week."

Addie could not feign exuberance at that moment. She knew full well that James would find a good job in Boston. He had seven meetings planned, all with seemingly good employers. He also had appointments with other former islanders who had moved to Boston. James certainly was going to make his time there productive.

Addie knew it was only a matter of time before she, too, was heading there. If only she could be happy about it.

The Boston Boat far exceeded James's expectations in terms of its travel schedule, meals, and accommodations—all quite good for the unexpectedly low ticket price. But the best part of the trip was meeting fellow islanders and hearing their stories. With the economic depression hitting Prince Edward Island so hard right now, families were gathering their belongings and heading to a better life in Boston.

James met other young men who were tradesmen and businessmen, and their stories were the same. They loved living on the island, but employment had dried up, and they had families to support.

It seemed from what he heard that many immigrants had settled in Boston, and there was quite a community of islanders among them. They liked Boston because the weather was similar to that of the island. The city was located on the ocean, featuring a large harbor. Numerous factories operated in various industries, including boot making, silk production, clothing, and more. Professionals could find job opportunities in many fields.

Best yet, there was always news from home since so many traveled back and forth from Prince Edward Island to Boston.

Boston proper had been growing since the 1800s. The city's access to a major harbor for shipping made it ideal for commerce, both within the States and internationally. Boston boasted numerous modes of transport, from horse-drawn buggies to electric streetcars, trains, countless means of water transport, and more. The city was bursting with hundreds of thousands of people living in its downtown.

James listened carefully to his fellow boatmates on his journey to Boston. He knew that a considerable number of Prince Edward Island immigrants lived in East Boston, Roslindale, and the Dorchester suburb of the city. All these areas provided easy access to the financial institutions in Boston proper.

James had planned to stay in a boardinghouse in East Boston for this trip, which would necessitate a daily ferry ride. He had also heard that a new tunnel was currently being constructed under Boston Harbor to speed up transport between the two destinations.

Addie would likely not be interested in tunnel or ferry transportation, so he would need to visit both Roslindale and Dorchester on this trip to learn more about lodgings for families with young children.

After the journey on the Boston Boat, James made his way to the East Boston ferry, which was located farther down the harbor docks. The ferry was teeming with young men and some women who were commuting back home after working in the city all day.

James was tired and was ready for a good night's rest. Tomorrow promised to be busy—he planned to meet with three different businesses about positions. He arranged all his meetings for the first three days of the visit; the latter part of the week would involve trips to Roslindale and Dorchester to explore available accommodations for his growing family.

Life takes many turns, Clara thought as she quietly observed her daughter retreating into the role of their child rather than being her usual independent self. Addie was in denial, and it was time to begin facing the circumstances head-on.

As a wife, mother, and accomplished professional writer, Addie needed to spread her wings and move forward with her husband.

Clara mused silently, *We pray for such concrete answers. "Please give me this, or don't do that," we beseech our angels. But discomfort can lead to growth.* Clara was well aware of that fact from her own life journey.

It was time for her youngest daughter to learn this as well.

While James was in Boston, Addie became a permanent fixture at Clara and Will's home. She would arrive with Rose right in time for breakfast and stay all day through dinner. If Clara and Will went to the store or the Charity House, Addie would set Rose down for her nap and settle in at the desk to write in her journal. She had been given few writing assignments lately and was beginning to realize that the job market did indeed seem to be a bit slow here on the island.

At the desk, however, Addie came to life. Her journal was not merely a record of her days; it was a narrative of her hopes and dreams for her young family.

When James first mentioned moving from Prince Edward Island, Addie was shocked. Their life here was so wonderful, so serene, so content. However, with no job prospects and her own work dwindling at the magazine, Addie was beginning to understand the need for a change.

"Today, I feel the winds of change," Addie began her journal entry on the third day James was away.

"James has now had a few productive meetings and will most likely come home soon with a plan for our move. It was good to talk to him last night; he had an excitement in his voice that I haven't heard in quite a few months. Perhaps this move will be as thrilling as he hopes for us."

Addie recounted her phone call with James last night. Will and Clara were among the first islanders to own a phone—first in the store and now in their house and Bill's apartment above the store. Although the call did not have the best reception, it played a vital role in helping Addie accept and understand her husband's plan.

She felt the baby move in her belly as she continued writing at the desk. This child might even be born in a new country! How odd that seemed, although now it was less frightful.

Addie put both hands on the desk, as if channeling its soul—if a desk could have a soul. She knew this desk had given her mother great strength all these years, and she prayed for strength herself to accept and embrace the journey ahead.

James had a highly productive trip to Boston. By the end of the second day, he had received two job offers, both from banks. He informed both banks that he would discuss it with his wife—the position with the greatest potential for advancement required him to start within two weeks. James understood that this would be challenging with the baby on the way, but his intuition suggested it was the right fit for their future.

With confidence in his future employment, James made his way to the Boston suburbs to learn more about the Prince Edward Island immigrant community and find suitable accommodations for his growing family.

Dorchester was immediately of interest to him. Just a quick streetcar ride from downtown Boston, where the financial institutions were located, Dorchester's wide streets and large homes with yards were a welcome sight. Most were two—and three—family dwellings, with children racing from yard to yard and a vibrant community of relocated Canadians, along with Irish, English, Italian, and other immigrants in various neighborhoods. Dorchester felt vibrant, diverse, and alive to James.

James met with a few families who had relocated and found a spacious two-bedroom apartment for rent on the second floor of a triple-decker. The home was occupied above and below by two different families from Prince Edward Island, with four toddlers and one newborn among them. Perfect for Addie to have some immediate companionship, James thought to himself. The streetcar was just a short walk from the dwelling and would provide access to and from Boston proper.

Now it was time to return home and discuss the future with Addie . . .

Addie was not surprised. She had been preparing for the inevitable for some time now, resigned to the change ahead, and braced herself for it. But the timeline was not what she had anticipated.

"Addie, I have found us a perfectly suitable apartment for our first year, and I am sure I have also chosen the right employment opportunity, thanks to your father and his outreach to his contacts," James said with an enthusiasm she had not heard in quite some time.

Addie was proud of James; this was a bold move he felt he had to make for her and their children. However, she wasn't prepared for what he said next: "And we must move within ten days, so I have the opportunity to help you settle in before I start at the bank the following Monday."

Ten days to move from the only place she had known as home? Leaving her beloved family and beautiful island? Her heart sank at the prospect.

"James, can we just have a bit more time?" she pleaded. James's response surprised her; his tone was firm and deliberate.

"Addie, this is in the best interests of our family. Your parents understand the importance of our independence and having our own lives. We have their full support, and I know that this is the right move for all of us. The timing may not be perfect, but there will never be a 'right' time. Please trust me; we will be happy in Boston."

Addie took a deep breath. The baby started kicking in her belly, and she could not help but laugh. Rose was looking forward to new Boston friends. James had already created a road map for the family there, and now their unborn child was weighing in on the move.

"It's meant to be," a soft voice whispered in her mind. She embraced James tightly and went to tell Clara and Will the plan.

The move to Boston was rather uneventful, and Addie was surprised by how smoothly everything went. They didn't bring much with them—just clothing and some of Rose's favorite toys. The new dwelling came furnished and would serve as a "first stop" for them as they acclimated to their new home.

Clara and Will felt sadness mingled with hope for the young family—the first and only Warren children to leave Prince Edward Island. Clara wanted to cry about her daughter's move, but deep down, she sensed it was for the best. James yearned to carve his own path in life, and Will recognized that he cast a long shadow over them.

Will felt relieved in many ways; the economic climate was poor, and he and Bill were doing everything they could to keep the family secure during this business downturn. Clara was also feeling the pinch, as there were significantly fewer tourism volunteer projects but a huge increase in the need for donations at the Caring House. Unfortunately, there were also fewer extra goods available to donate.

It was a challenging time on the island, but Clara and Will knew that if they remained prudent, they could weather the storm. If only Will's energy weren't so low.

Every day was becoming more challenging. He often felt winded from the moment he woke up, needing to sit and catch his breath frequently. He had been living with his diagnosis for many years now, with no real cure available. Clara was deeply concerned, yet she was mindful that they were fortunate Will had survived for so long.

The day James, Addie, and Rose departed for Boston, Clara decided it was time for another novena attempt. Will was failing, and Clara needed him now more than ever in her life. She could not bear the thought of losing Will, but perhaps Saint Martha would be the answer.

That evening, Clara went to the desk and took the perfectly folded piece of paper from its secret spot. She opened it and looked at her handwriting, which had faded over the years.

I'll set off to church tomorrow—it's Tuesday—and begin again, she thought to herself. *But I will go to the Catholic church this time, as it feels like the right fit for my prayers at this particular time.*

With that, she put the novena in her purse and went to bed, dreaming of her daughter in Boston.

The following weeks were busy, but Clara dedicated each Tuesday to stealthily entering the local Catholic church to pray the novena. By timing her visits a few hours after morning Mass, Clara ensured she was always the only person inside each week.

She would leave Will at home or at the store, kiss his

forehead, and head out on her mission—to pray for his well-being. Will had no idea that Clara was doing this. He was often so tired that his concentration was not as it used to be. Clara was saddened as she watched him slowly fade away before her eyes.

Martha listened intently to Clara's pleas.

Clara was incredibly special. Martha marveled at her transformation over the years—from a sad, lonely daughter to a heartbroken soldier's wife, to a young widow with a child, and finally to a mother who lost her firstborn. Yet, through it all, Clara remained graceful, loving, and dignified.

She never lost sight of what she had rather than what she had lost. Clara lived each day with spirit, always striving to help others. She was truly an inspiration.

Clara and Will had a magnificent bond. Each had a vibrant life force, but combined, they seemed able to overcome anything. Clara was not willing to give up. There had to be an answer, and Martha indeed heard her prayers.

Addie was surprised by Boston. Although she missed her family terribly, there was something special about this city. There were many new faces and friends, and Rose quickly had little toddlers to play with each day.

Addie was moving through her pregnancy; it was a bit different than her first, but she had plenty of energy and was looking forward to the baby's arrival. The neighborhood was buzzing with new arrivals from Canada, Ireland, and Scotland. Just a few blocks away, there were entire neighborhoods filled with other groups of newcomers. As so many of the residents were also new to the area, it was easy to make acquaintances.

As the last of six children and much younger than her siblings, Addie had led a quiet life primarily with her mother and father. For the first time, she found herself surrounded by others her own age and place in life, living away from her homeland without the comforting presence of her parents. While she adored both ways of life, she was beginning to understand that this period of separation was a crucial part of her journey toward becoming her own woman.

James quickly adapted to his new position. He enjoyed taking the streetcar to work each morning and loved the bustle of downtown Boston, which reminded him of the city life he had left behind to bring his parents to Prince Edward Island. James felt proud of his decision and equally proud of Addie and her willingness to embrace this new city and country.

Within a few months of settling in, Warren Leonard Ryan was born at Massachusetts General Hospital in downtown Boston, one of the state's first hospitals. James and Addie were delighted—they now had a boy and a girl—as their dreams were indeed coming true.

CHAPTER 10

New Beginnings

*T*here are times in life when we don't understand why things happen, and times when we feel as if we have no control. As she thought these words to herself, Clara reflected that what we *can* control is how we respond—whether we are happy with the change or not. For Clara, rising to the occasion was not just a noble thing to do; it was the only thing to do.

Clara and Addie wrote to each other regularly and indulged in phone calls as often as possible. Addie had to use the phone line on the first level of the house; she called Clara and Will every other morning before they began their day. Clara never mentioned Will's declining health; she did not want to make Addie feel badly for not being there with them.

Their four other children and spouses—along with many adorable grandchildren—were with them daily to cheer them up and help keep Will's mind occupied beyond his fading energy. However, as much as Clara adored all her children, the bond between her and Addie was strong. They had spent so much time together when Addie was a child, and Clara missed her youngest in a sad, yet accepting way.

"Is Father able to get out to the store often?" Addie would inquire on their phone calls.

"Yes, whenever he sees fit. You know how much he enjoys being in the store with the family and our customers," Clara would attempt to respond cheerfully.

Addie could hear the ping of melancholy in her mother's voice. She knew in her heart that her father's health was poor. It had been a miracle that Will had been able to function as well as he had all these years.

Yet Addie knew that more could be done to help her father. She had delivered her newborn, Warren, in a large hospital in Boston, staffed by the best doctors in the States. Perhaps someone could see her father and help relieve his exhaustion. She made a note to contact her physician to inquire.

The following Monday, Addie called her doctor, who was affiliated with Massachusetts General Hospital, a large facility located in Boston's West End.

"Well, Addie, I do indeed know an excellent heart specialist here at the hospital," Dr. McRoy stated during their call.

"It seems your father has managed this condition for quite some time, which is commendable for a man of his age," he continued. "Let's see if we can schedule an appointment for him with Dr. Pulin, one of our top specialists, in the coming weeks."

Addie could not thank Dr. McRoy enough. Her father's care consisted mainly of rest and inactivity, paired with a "healthy diet" prescribed by his personal physician on the island. Addie believed that the medical care in one of the larger cities in the States would likely be more beneficial for her father.

Clara and Will agreed to come to Boston to see the specialist. They did, however, have a small request: that their beautiful collie, Millie, accompany them. Millie was a gift from their sons, Bill and John, who purchased her during a trip to England two years earlier. Queen Victoria had loved collies, which contributed to their popularity in England. The boys believed that a beautiful, well-trained dog would be a wonderful companion for their parents, and Millie had not disappointed. She was an athletic dog who required a good walk each day, which was part of Will's health routine.

Will, Clara, and Millie took the Boston Boat on a sunny June weekend from Prince Edward Island to Boston Harbor. James and Addie, along with toddler Rose and baby Warren, were all waiting at the dock, waving, smiling, and literally bursting with joy.

James cherished his in-laws and felt they were like his own parents. He was very thankful for all that Will had done to assist them with their move, and he was equally grateful to Clara for permitting Addie to relocate to Boston with her blessing.

The handsome older couple, accompanied by their stunning dog, slowly navigated through the crowd into the exuberant embrace of the four Ryans.

"We are so happy you are here!" Addie exclaimed, tears of joy streaming down her cheeks. James stood by her side, cradling Warren in his arms, while Rose clapped her hands in delight, welcoming her beloved grandparents.

"Grammy and Grandpa, welcome to Boston," Rose announced with an ear-to-ear smile on her sweet, round face, her curly brown locks flowing in the harbor breeze.

Clara and Will were happy to have arrived, but they were exhausted from their trip. The family headed back to the apartment, where Addie had prepared the children's room for her parents. The four Ryans would make do sleeping together in the master bedroom—a small sacrifice to have Rose's parents here with them.

The hope for better medical care for Will was the unspoken prayer that everyone held, but no one spoke about the true reason for the visit.

"Heart failure has been a condition since the time of the Romans," Dr. Pulin explained to Will. "We don't have a specific cure for it, but we are offering several treatments here at the hospital that may help alleviate some of your symptoms."

Doctor Pulin was impressed by the lifestyle that Will and Clara maintained on the island. Their diet mainly consisted of fresh fish, vegetables, and seasonal island produce. Even with his heart condition, Will went to the store each day and walked as much as he could. These were all crucial measures to combat the disease.

Will took a deep breath. The past few years had been

difficult, and he found it impossible to conceal his fatigue from Clara. However, he would not let his condition define him; he lived for Clara and his family. His mental strength provided him with the physical strength to keep moving forward. He was also relieved to be in a medical facility where his condition was well understood and studied. He harbored hope for the future.

Clara was also hopeful—for what the doctor might prescribe and that Martha had heard her pleas, promising to keep Will safe and with her.

Doctor Pulin had a plan. The use of simple diuretics to alleviate the fluid retention associated with heart disease was providing relief to many patients. While not a cure, these medications could often help with the fatigue and discomfort. If that method offered no relief, it might also be possible for Will to undergo treatment with a fluid drainage protocol.

"Let's begin with a small dose of the medication and a few additional changes to your diet, then we'll see how you feel from there. I also want you to walk daily in the fresh sea air, as this will benefit your spirits as much as your heart," Doctor Pulin advised. "And, Will, I'd like to see you every two weeks over the next few months to monitor your progress."

Will and Clara exchanged glances. This was not a death sentence. It might not be a foolproof cure either, but anything that could help Will regain some of his strength would be greatly appreciated. However, they also realized that they could not remain in Addie and James's small quarters for several months. Their lodging arrangement needed some adjustments.

Clara looked up at the sky that afternoon, searching the clouds for a sign from Martha. Would her prayers be answered? Or had they already been? It was impossible to truly know at that moment.

Addie and James were pleased with the medical visit—and the prognosis. Addie was especially happy that her parents would be staying in Boston for a few months. Everyone agreed that Will and Clara should look for a new place, as the family was bursting at the seams in their two-bedroom home.

James was just as delighted as Addie that her parents were with them. He had a deep affinity for them; they were so different from his own family, and he thrived in their presence, soaking up their calming love and support.

Clara still marveled at how much James reminded her of her sweet son Christian. Addie had chosen well—James was a quiet, confident, and caring husband and father who prioritized his family above all else. She pondered what Christian might have been like and how his life may have unfolded if he hadn't passed away at such a young age.

"Hold your sadness lightly, Clara—Christian is always with you, as are Arthur and your parents," the voice whispered in her mind. "For today, focus on what you have before you and cherish each day with those you hold dear." The voice was comforting yet firm. Clara always wondered where these thoughts originated—was it her own consciousness soothing her, or could it be something more? Might Martha be nearby?

She patted Millie's soft head and took out her journal. She still journaled every day; it had become a ritual that calmed her soul. But Clara missed her desk—writing there felt like a spiritual experience for her. It allowed her to connect with her past through the smooth wood that Arthur had crafted into a handsome desk, a place where she could engage in the most magical thinking about both the past and the present.

Addie's simple work desk was positioned in the center of the apartment's living room, where a large typewriter occupied much of the workspace. Clara glanced at the typewriter with pen in hand. Although she had not mastered the art of typing like her daughter, she still enjoyed putting pen to paper, spending hours crafting her journal entries.

But Addie was in a new world now; she had recently submitted some of her past magazine articles to the *Boston Globe* and had been brought on as a contributor. Typing was essential for her.

Clara was thrilled for her daughter, now a mother of two beautiful children, married to a wonderful man, and pursuing her passion—writing. It was a bond between mother and daughter—the joy of observing, feeling, and composing. What a gift it was for them both.

The hunt for a residence for Will and Clara in Dorchester was fruitful. They didn't require too much—just a one-bedroom apartment on the first floor to ease the strain of stairs for Will and provide quick access to the outdoors for Millie.

They discovered a charming spot on the first level of a three-decker house near Franklin Park, which would serve as an excellent walking venue. The home was about a ten-minute stroll from Addie and James's apartment, although their family was already contemplating a move to larger accommodations.

Clara and Will's apartment came furnished with a suitable kitchen, a cozy living room that featured a small table and chair, and a bedroom. Clara gazed at the makeshift table in dismay. She truly needed a more stable desk for her daily journaling. Her thoughts turned to her beloved desk in Prince Edward Island; how would she manage without it for the coming months?

Will was satisfied with the accommodation; Dorchester was a vibrant suburb, and the streetcar was just steps away, making it easy for them to reach Massachusetts General Hospital for his regular checkups. However, the store, their extended family, and the allure of the red sand cliffs of Prince Edward Island were always in his dreams.

Will dutifully followed Dr. Pulin's orders regarding his health. The excess fluid gradually eased from his body, and his energy improved. After two months, Will asked when he and Clara might be able to head back home.

"Will, I am very pleased with your progress, but I would prefer to keep you under my care a bit longer. The journey to Prince Edward Island is lengthy, and the hospital facilities there are not as advanced as they are here in Boston. I understand that this may not be what you wanted to hear, but I hope you will consider my advice in this matter," Doctor Pulin asserted with conviction.

Will was not pleased. He missed the shop and the family, and he missed the essence of Prince Edward Island. Although the Boston weather reminded them of home, the hustle and bustle of the city was not something he or Clara relished. Addie and James were thriving here, but Clara and Will yearned for the natural beauty and tranquility of their island home.

Another month passed. Clara began seeking out some volunteer work to make better use of her time in Boston— and she persuaded Will to join her in finding a meaningful way to engage with the community while in Dorchester.

James was quickly establishing a reputation for himself in the city's financial sector. He thoroughly enjoyed being engaged in the daily life of the vibrant Boston business community. Addie, now pregnant with their third child, was busy with the children and writing articles for the newspaper. There were countless stories to cover in Boston. Many of her writings focused on the city's cultural events, including reports on exhibitions at the Museum of Fine Arts and the nearby Isabella Stewart Gardner Museum.

Although Addie and James would have appreciated Clara and Will helping with their growing family, the young couple understood that their older counterparts needed something for themselves while they were in town.

"Mother, the First Methodist Episcopal church has numerous programs where you and Father could lend a hand. Many immigrants from different countries are arriving here and need help settling in. Perhaps you could assist as you did with Christian's Caring House back home?" Addie mentioned to her parents at dinner.

James chimed in, "Will, you could bring a lot of knowledge regarding procurement of goods that newcomers might need, and the church always needs help with fundraising and managing its donations. Clara, perhaps you could assist with the clothing and bedding donation activities."

Will seemed pleased with this idea. However, Clara had another thought in mind. While she enjoyed her volunteer work at the Caring House, she truly thrived when involved in her tourism promotional activities. Perhaps Boston would have some needs in that area for her to explore. However, if she were to stay much longer, she would need her desk. She made a note to discuss this with Will.

Will settled into a weekly—and later nearly daily—routine of helping at the church. He enjoyed hearing the stories of those arriving in Boston, learning more about what they had left behind and what they hoped for in the future.

His regular check-ins with Dr. Pulin were now monthly, which allowed him much more free time to devote to what was becoming quite a passion. Will and Clara frequently talked with the family back on Prince Edward Island. Will was pleased that the store appeared to be running smoothly, and the family was happy that he was feeling better and enjoying his time in the States.

Addie and James had recently purchased a home of their own on Chickatawbut Street in Dorchester. It was a two-story, single-family home with a small yard on a tree-lined street where many families were relocating.

They were fortunate to be able to afford a home thanks to James's advancements at work, and they were thrilled to have more room for their growing family. The only drawback was that the house was over three miles from Will and Clara's apartment.

"Why don't you and Father come back to live with us for a while?" Addie implored. "We love having you here, and Millie will enjoy our backyard. It's too far to walk from where you are now, and the streetcar isn't a direct route to your home from ours."

Will and Clara thanked Addie for the generous invitation, but the two were content living on their own, even though both felt that their current apartment wasn't exactly what they were seeking.

Will secretly discussed a plan with his sons to surprise Clara. The boys would send her desk to Dorchester, shipping it to Boston from the island, where it would arrive in a few weeks. Will had also convinced Clara that they should start looking for a larger place to stay.

Clara enjoyed living in the Boston area, but she did not love it by any means. Nevertheless, she had heard about other places in Massachusetts that sounded interesting. When she inquired about volunteering in tourism, she discovered regions of the state that were beginning to promote themselves as tourist destinations—similar to the work she had done on Prince Edward Island.

The island of Martha's Vineyard was mentioned to Clara. Located just a few miles off the coast, steamship ferries transported many summer vacationers who often fell in love with the island and purchased property. Clara was intrigued.

"Will, I would like to visit Martha's Vineyard," Clara announced as they took their daily afternoon walk with Millie to the park. "I've done some research, and it sounds rather similar to Prince Edward Island. Martha's Vineyard is actively promoting tourism, highlighting the healthy living qualities of island life, such as fresh sea air, tranquility, and natural beauty. Doesn't that sound familiar?" She laughed.

Will gazed at her with curiosity. This woman always amazed him; her adventurous spirit and thirst for knowledge never faded. Clara radiated joy as she shared her idea with Will, and he found himself loving her even more, captivated by her enthusiasm steering them forward.

"As I just met with Dr. Pulin last week, I have no obligations I can't postpone. Let's take a trip and learn more about Martha's Vineyard."

With that, Clara began looking for travel and hotel arrangements to the Vineyard. Millie would stay with Addie and James as soon as Clara could explain the new plan to them.

Getting to Martha's Vineyard was a bit more complicated than Will and Clara had anticipated. The steamship ferry departed from New Bedford, Massachusetts, a whaling town about fifty miles from Boston. They purchased train tickets to New Bedford, and from there, they would take the ferry across the sound to the island. Once they reached the island, they would need to hire a horse and buggy to take them to their hotel in Edgartown. Automobiles were a rarity on the Vineyard.

Addie felt puzzled by her parents' new adventure.

"Why on earth would you go to Martha's Vineyard? It's so small and isolated. What if something happened to Father there? Did you discuss this with Dr. Pulin?" she asked Clara frantically.

Clara understood Addie's concern. However, once the plan was set, Will became very excited about the adventure. He was eager to explore more of the new world they were now living in, and his health had stabilized. Will felt alive again, and he was thrilled to see Clara enthusiastic as well.

It was time for them to explore new possibilities—while they still had the chance. Neither of them would be convinced otherwise.

Will and Clara arranged a call with Dr. Pulin, who believed a week's trip to Martha's Vineyard would be fine since Will's health had stabilized. He pointed out that there was a marine hospital on the island in case of an emergency and mentioned that the island was much closer to Boston than returning to Prince Edward Island. Clara and Will were pleased to hear Dr. Pulin's thoughts on the visit and hoped the information would ease their daughter's mind.

Clara had chosen The Harbor View Hotel as their weeklong stay for the trip. When this grand hotel opened, more than four hundred guests attended its opening gala. Clara had read about the hotel and believed it was a central hub for any tourism activities the island might offer.

The summer season marked the peak of tourism, especially in places like Martha's Vineyard. However, it was also crucial to attract visitors year-round to keep the locals employed. Clara and Will had extensive experience in this area and believed that they might still have something to contribute, even in their "golden years."

Without a second thought, they packed two suitcases, took Millie to Addie's home, and boarded the train to New Bedford. The ride was uneventful, and they arrived at the New Bedford harbor about two hours before the steamship ferry to Martha's Vineyard.

Clara noticed Addie's disapproving gaze as they left the Boston train station, but Millie quickly drew the attention of Rose and Warren, providing an excellent distraction.

The ferry ride was magnificent. June was a crisp month in the Boston States, warmer than Prince Edward Island, but with a cool breeze each day. The sun shone brightly, dancing off the ocean waters as the ferry navigated through the Cape Cod Canal on its way to Martha's Vineyard. From New Bedford, it was over twenty nautical miles to the island. On the deck of the ferry, Clara and Will could see the beautiful silhouette of the Vineyard—

sandy beaches and bluffs, some of red clay not unlike their beloved Prince Edward Island.

Something about this journey resonated with both of them. While they enjoyed being near Addie and Will in Dorchester, their souls craved island life. They laughed to themselves, wondering who on earth would seek their volunteer advice at their age—two older folks from another country in the Boston States due to medical reasons. Yet they also knew that, together, they had much to offer anyone who might be interested. They made a great team, and they recognized it. Saint Martha was aware of it as well.

The ferry docked in Cottage City, a magical village with an expansive town common. Clara could hardly believe her eyes; there before them was an array of gingerbread houses scattered throughout the village, looking as if they had emerged straight from the fairy tales she had read as a child. They disembarked from the ferry and proceeded to the center of town.

The island community was vibrant. The Flying Horses Carousel, as it was named, spun round and round, delighting the children who rode its colorful wooden horses. Clara read about the history of this whimsical attraction; it had been moved to the island in 1884 and featured expertly crafted, hand-carved wooden horses with manes and tails made of real horsehair and striking glass eyes. How Rose and even Warren would love to see this, Clara mused. Will, equally impressed by the charming town, had gone to hire a buggy to take them to Edgartown, where their hotel was located.

The ride from Cottage City to Edgartown was lovely; it meandered along the coastline, where Clara and Will marveled at the red clay bluffs, which were so reminiscent of their homeland. The island featured rolling meadows and lush farmlands, all framed by the sparkling deep blue sea. The clouds drifted across the vibrant blue sky as if they were dancing.

If you looked closely, you could see entire stories unfolding in the sky—Clara spotted a passing cloud that resembled Millie, and Will was sure he could see the sail of a ship being pushed by the wind in another cloud formation. Clara had always understood the enchantment of the clouds and sky. Today, she felt its power more than she had in a very long time.

While Cottage City exuded a charming summer camp ambience—indeed, it was a camp for Methodist churchgoers—Edgartown presented a decidedly more formal atmosphere. This settlement, home to numerous whaling ship captains, featured historic houses that faced the harbor, allowing wives to watch for their husbands' return from roof platforms atop the home. Recently, the Edgartown Yacht Club opened its doors, becoming a central hub of social activity in the village.

The Harbor View Hotel was a grand dame, situated directly across from the Edgartown lighthouse, which was easily accessible via a rose-lined walk down to the hard-packed sand pathway. The hotel's large, covered porch was ideal for viewing ships as the sun set over the petite red cliffs of nearby Chappaquiddick Island. Large and small single-family homes lined the street leading to the hotel from the center of Edgartown.

Will and Clara were besotted by the entire island. Edgartown reminded them of Charlottetown, with Martha's Vineyard resembling the United States' own version of Prince Edward Island.

"Do you feel it, Clara? There's something here for us. I don't know how or why, but the premonition is overwhelming to me."

"Yes, Will, I do. It's in the air, in the sky, in the clouds above. The magic we've been so sorely missing is right here."

Martha silently watched Clara and Will from her perch in the lighthouse and smiled. The journey may not have been what Clara had prayed for; it had been filled with both joys and sorrows, but it had brought them here. Which was exactly where they were meant to be.

The visit to the Vineyard went better than planned. The two enjoyed exploring Edgartown and learned more about the island. They visited the awe-inspiring red clay cliffs of Aquinnah, located on the far west side of Martha's Vineyard. Will went fishing, Clara delved deeper into the island's history, and together they explored the ministry campgrounds, and more.

Through his connections, Will arranged a meeting with the local bank that was most involved in the island's tourism efforts. The bank's president, Thomas Worth, a descendant of a longtime Vineyard family, was pleased to meet them.

As Will and Clara were only seeking volunteer positions, the conversation was open and lively. What surprised them was Mr. Worth's sincere interest in their extensive experience managing a company while simultaneously launching a charity on a small island. Clara's work in tourism was also an advantageous aspect of the couple's background. After what felt like thirty minutes of engaging conversation, they realized almost two hours had gone by.

"My goodness, I'm sorry to have kept you so long! I should let you enjoy the rest of your day. However, I want to say one more thing before you leave. Now, I realize that the two of you are living in Boston, but we could really use some help year-round here on the island if you would consider a temporary relocation," Thomas Worth explained.

"It's a special place here on Martha's Vineyard, and we could truly benefit from individuals like you who are knowledgeable in commerce and tourism. I realize you're not seeking full-time employment, but perhaps a mentorship arrangement might appeal to you. In return for your support, we could offer you accommodations while aiding my team and our fellow business partners here on the island. I know it's a great deal to consider, so I will let you think it over and get back to me with your decision."

Clara and Will were pleasantly surprised. They would need to speak with Dr. Pulin and the family, but this new opportunity held tremendous appeal.

Back in Dorchester, James and Addie were settling into their new home and having a delightful time watching Millie. They had never considered having a dog in the past but having Millie in the family, even if just for this one week, made them rethink the idea of having a furry companion of their own.

After dinner the night before picking up Clara and Will at the train station, the phone rang. As Addie walked into the living room to answer it, she marveled at how wonderful it was to have their spacious new home—complete with their own phone!

"Hello, sweet Addie," Clara said lovingly. "How are you, James, and the family? We hope Millie hasn't been too much of a bother for you."

"Mother, we just adore her! If you didn't love her so much, we'd steal her away from you," Addie joked.

"I'm so happy to hear that, darling. We were hoping you could watch her for another week so we can stay here on the Vineyard to sort out a few details."

Addie was perplexed. Work out a few details? What was her mother talking about?

"What kind of 'details' are you working on, Mother? We thought you were just going for a short vacation before moving closer to us."

Clara took a deep breath. With Will by her side, she slowly explained that they had simply fallen in love with the island and hoped to spend more time there. They shared their new mentorship roles and detailed the lovely little home that the bank president insisted they stay in, just down the street from their current hotel. It had been in his family for generations and was currently unoccupied. The house was warm and inviting, and from the small backyard, one could see the Edgartown lighthouse. They adored the home and felt they could make a difference on the Vineyard.

They had already spoken with Dr. Pulin. The decision was to stay for three weeks at a time, then travel back to Boston for Will's monthly checkups. The journey each month was much shorter than the time it would take for them to travel back and forth from Prince Edward Island. They would return from the Vineyard to Dorchester for a few nights before each doctor's visit and perhaps stay in the guest room on the second floor of Addie and James's new home.

Addie sighed. There was never any stopping her parents, and she had no intention of trying. She hadn't told Clara yet that the desk had arrived at the house; it was meant to be a surprise.

After the call—and after calling her siblings to share the news—James and Addie set about preparing the guest room and placing the desk in the alcove at the base of the stairs leading to the second floor.

The light was lovely as it streamed through a small window in the stairwell. Clara would truly enjoy journaling there when she visited them, and for now, Addie would keep the desk company by writing in this cherished spot.

Saint Martha was pleased that Will and Clara had discovered the Vineyard. She had always loved its breathtaking beauty and serene landscapes. Martha understood that this enchanting island would nourish their spirits and offer solace during this chapter of their lives. Here, they could rejuvenate and heal.

Martha fondly reflected on the history of this enchanting island. She smiled knowingly as she recalled the many legends of Martha's Vineyard. According to the stories, the origin of the name has always been somewhat of a mystery. Some tales suggest that, in the early 1600s, English explorer Bartholomew Gosnold named it after his daughter. Others propose that he might have named it after his mother-in-law, who shared the same name. Or perhaps Thomas Mayhew's daughter, Martha, inspired the name when he purchased the island in the mid-1600s.

Saint Martha, renowned for her hospitality, had a good inkling of the name's origin; the most popular theory suggests that early settlers named the island Martha's Vineyard because they viewed it as a hospitable place. With a knowing smile, Martha reflected on the generations of islanders who had called this sacred ground home. She felt delighted that Clara and Will would now become part of its history.

CHAPTER 11

Growth

*L*ife moves like the wind, changing direction at a moment's notice, pushing us in one direction or creating a force we must brace for as we seek to move forward. Clara's thoughts raced. She believed in the power of change; if embraced, it could lead to positive outcomes.

Clara and Will loved living on Martha's Vineyard. It was so similar to their beloved Prince Edward Island, yet as part of the American States, there was so much to discover. The two especially enjoyed their time there during the "offseason," when the island consisted mainly of locals, with few tourists. This was quiet time, wonderful for relaxation—but not so helpful for the island's economy. Clara and Will aimed to enhance tourism during the fall and early spring months, and the two were excited about their plans.

The more they learned of the island and its history, the more they fell in love with it. The people were remarkable; the population was diverse, consisting of settlers from Europe, Indigenous peoples, and summer Methodist campers attracting a growing number of African Americans. The island was even a stop on the Underground Railroad during the Civil War in the States. Clara and Will enjoyed hearing stories from the new people they encountered, with Clara keeping a journal of their intriguing tales.

Clara was fascinated to discover the sizable deaf population on the island. Just fifty years earlier, nearly one in twenty-five residents in the town of Chilmark, located "up island," was deaf. Both deaf and hearing residents utilized Martha's Vineyard Sign Language (MVSL), which eliminated deafness as a barrier in the community. Clara and Will were learning MVSL to engage with the hearing-impaired islanders, most of whom were quite independent.

"One day, I might write a book about this place," Clara would tell Will during their daily walks with Millie. "The world needs to learn more about this peaceful, beautiful oasis that is welcoming to so many."

"If you want to author a book, my dear Clara, I know you will. There's no stopping you once you get an idea in that pretty head of yours," Will said knowingly as the three strolled down North Water Street in Edgartown.

Millie was in heaven on the island. It had been hard to pull her away from the loving embrace of Rose and Warren, and even Addie tried to persuade her parents to let Millie stay with them when they left Dorchester.

"Millie is the ideal companion for the children, Mother. And if Rose has to endure the sadness of missing her grandparents, at least Millie will be here to soften the blow."

Clara accepted none of it; she adored Millie and was thrilled that her sons had brought her back from England. It was the most thoughtful gift she had ever received, apart from Arthur's desk. Millie was Clara's constant companion, bringing immense joy. She sparked conversation whenever they took her for walks—each passerby wanted to pet her or hold her paw, which she would gently place in the palm of anyone who asked.

"Addie, I'm not sure what you'll miss more—Millie, your father, me, or the desk!" Clara said as she and Will—with Millie in tow—prepared to move the desk to the Vineyard. The desk was the only piece of furniture they brought from Dorchester, as the charming island home had come furnished. Clara needed the desk; she felt she must take it with her—it belonged with her on this magical Martha's Vineyard.

Saint Martha was content; watching Will and Clara explore her namesake island brought her immense joy. Their inquisitive, always helpful and hopeful attitudes were utterly amazing. Their souls kept growing, learning, and giving. She could not wait to see what they would do next.

Back in her new home in Dorchester, Addie shrugged. Her dream had been to have her parents close by, but now she only saw them a few nights a month when Will came to Boston to visit Dr. Pulin.

Pregnant with her third child, she felt a bit overwhelmed with Rose and Warren and worried about how she would manage with a newborn while maintaining her writing. Letting go of her passion was not something she planned to do—it nourished her soul, and she was determined to figure out a way to continue writing, even as the mother of three young children. However, her parents' move made everything a bit more challenging.

"Addie, have you considered getting some domestic help after the baby arrives?" James asked. Addie was unsure how to reply. She had never contemplated hiring someone to assist with her children or household chores. This idea was entirely foreign to her.

"I understand that you wish your mother could be here helping with the children, but your parents must prioritize what is best for them. Living on the Vineyard appears to have brought them immense joy—and energy! Your father seems healthier than he has in years."

James continued with his suggestion. "Several of my coworkers have nannies who assist with their children, while others employ domestic help for cleaning and cooking. We now have a large home, and I believe it would greatly benefit us to bring in someone—whatever their role—to help."

James had made his case.

At first, Addie felt insulted by the offer—was it obvious that she could not manage two children, a large home, getting dinner on the table, and writing a feature article or two each month? She thought she had been handling it fairly well, but she was bone tired these days—most likely from the pregnancy, she thought, though a newborn was sure to add to the exhaustion.

"I will consider it, James. I feel somewhat uncomfortable with this idea, but I will entertain it."

With that, Addie finished setting the table for dinner and sat down at her typewriter while dinner roasted in the oven. Rose and Warren played with a toy train set on the floor nearby, while James changed out of his work clothing in their bedroom.

Addie loved her family and her life in Boston, and her work played a significant role in her happiness. She had encountered many interesting people in the city while covering museum collections and meeting visiting artists and musicians, among others. Giving up her work would be heartbreaking for her. Perhaps James was right; a little assistance with the house and children was exactly what she needed.

James was pleased that Addie was considering hiring someone to alleviate some of the burden. The children were both young—Rose was now five, and Warren was two and a half. The new baby, while a joyful addition, would add to Addie's already abundant plate.

James did what he could to support Addie. However, he worked long hours and was advancing quickly at work. He wanted Addie to be both happy as a mother and a writer, and he aimed to be an understanding father and husband. His own sad childhood weighed heavily on him, and he had no intention of being a selfish tyrant like his father.

James allowed himself to think about his family for a moment. His siblings reported that his mother was doing well in Quebec. She had her own small apartment and enjoyed visiting them and her grandchildren often.

James's father was another case. He had ended up in jail as expected and had five years left on his sentence. James wrote to him occasionally, but his father was furious that James had moved to the Boston States and referred to him as a "traitor" to his siblings. James sighed. There was nothing he could do except move on with his life and appreciate the blessings of his own family.

James set aside his sad feelings about his past. It was time to focus on the future; he would speak with Clara about Addie and her need for additional help once the baby arrived. He made a note to call her privately the next day to discuss the situation.

Clara enjoyed learning sign language and was picking it up at a much faster pace than Will. This island community was incredibly inclusive. Everyone seemed to communicate easily with one another, regardless of their disabilities.

"Clara, how are you signing so quickly? I can hardly keep up with you," Will lamented after an encounter in Edgartown with a lovely family that had both hearing and non-hearing members. "You all were signing so fast I missed half the conversation."

Clara gazed lovingly at her husband of over four decades. "We each have our talents, dear Will; this is just one of mine. But I assure you that your cup overflows with your own unique abilities." And she meant every word.

What she had not mentioned was that she was discussing Addie's need for a helper back in Dorchester, and the family's oldest daughter, Jane, was extremely interested in living off the island. Clara could not think of a more perfect young woman to live with Addie and James; now she simply had to introduce everyone and teach the Dorchester family Martha's Vineyard Sign Language.

Addie had not been well for a few days before she unexpectedly went into labor early one evening. The pains came quickly, and she knew immediately that the baby was on the way. James accompanied her to Massachusetts General Hospital to deliver the baby, rushing Rose and Warren to one of the neighbors for a sleepover since Clara and Will could not arrive in time to stay with the children.

Clara was quite worried; Addie had delivered the baby nearly four weeks early, and although this was her third child, she had given birth later than her due date for the other two. Clara quickly prepared for herself, Will, and Millie to return to Dorchester on the first available steamship ferry.

"I don't know, Will; I'm nervous about this baby. Something tells me there might be a problem."

Knowing his wife as he did and considering her intuitive abilities, Will also became concerned. Clara and Will's children had all experienced healthy, full-term births, and it had never crossed his mind that there could be a problem with a baby being born too early. Addie had been due in just over a month. Could there be serious issues with a birth occurring so much earlier than the baby's due date?

Will halted his mental spiral and promptly began packing. They might need to remain in Dorchester longer than they had initially planned.

At the hospital, Addie felt anxious. The baby seemed so vibrant, always kicking and making his or her presence known to her. But when her water broke unexpectedly, she experienced a pang of despair—she was due in a month's time, and her two other pregnancies had gone two weeks past their due dates. What if something was wrong with this precious soul within her?

"Stay calm, ma'am. We will help you deliver this baby," said the nurse assigned to Addie. Addie was feeling unwell; the contractions were coming rapidly now, and she sensed that the baby's birth was imminent.

"Deep breaths and a big push," the nurse encouraged. Addie did everything she could, knowing it was crucial to bring the child into the world as quickly as possible.

James was anxious. He and Addie approached this pregnancy as if it were a foregone conclusion that the baby would be healthy and vibrant, just like their two previous children. He had never thought of an early delivery and its potential impact on the child's health. His voice trembled when he called Clara that morning to inform her of the baby's early arrival.

Fortunately, Clara answered right away and instinctively realized that Addie needed her as soon as possible. Clara and Will were on their way, and James and Addie required their love and support now more than ever.

Four hours later, before Clara and Will arrived, Teddy Christian Ryan was born. His breathing was steady, but his complexion was jaundiced. Addie fought back tears as she set her eyes on her little boy. The yellow tone of his complexion was frightening to both her and James. They greeted baby Teddy for the first time, after which he was whisked away for the doctors to evaluate.

It felt like an eternity while the doctors examined Teddy. However, Addie's doctor returned to the room in just a few minutes with the newborn swaddled in his arms.

"This little fellow is definitely a fighter," Doctor Jeffries calmly reported. "He's a bit small, but he's healthy. He will need breast milk—often, as it's the best solution for newborn jaundice. Addie, we will keep you and Teddy here for a week to ensure that he is getting the milk he needs."

Addie and James breathed simultaneous sighs of relief as little Teddy was gently placed in Addie's arms. He was beautiful. The couple was smitten with their little miracle boy and looked forward to introducing him to his siblings and grandparents in the days ahead. They were incredibly thankful that support was on its way; Teddy would require a great deal of care in the first few months, and Addie would need as much help as possible.

As she gazed at her new child, Addie thought of her brother Christian. This little boy, whose middle name would always remind her of her beloved brother, appeared to resemble him in many ways. *I miss you so much, dear Christian. This namesake of yours will bring comfort to me, Mother, and Father; I just know it. He was meant to be here. Rest in peace, dear brother.*

Saint Martha, situated just outside the hospital room window, gazed in at the loving family. Christian had sent her a message for Addie that she would make sure was delivered very soon.

With the desk relocated to the Vineyard, Martha needed to be creative about how the message would be found. She would return to James and Addie's house while it was still empty and carefully place the message in a location for Addie to discover.

Martha arrived at the charming home on Chickatawbut Street a few minutes later. She felt proud of Addie and James for their ability to purchase such an enchanting property—a single-family Colonial-era house with four bedrooms, providing plenty of room for their growing family. The house featured wooden shingles and an attached barn that many homeowners now used to store their automobiles.

Addie fell in love with the home at first sight. The way the house was positioned on the lot maximized sunlight, creating a cheerful ambience. The yard, though small, was well-maintained and provided a delightful play space for the children.

As she glided through the home, Martha stopped at the spot where Clara's desk had been for a few short months. Addie had since purchased a desk of her own that occupied the space—it was a smaller, more modern version of a secretary's desk with a larger desktop to accommodate her typewriter and numerous research papers. The family telephone was also on the desk. From this carefully chosen position on the first level of the house, Addie could work while watching the children and easily move to and from the kitchen or outside into the backyard.

Christian, I believe you know precisely where I should place this note, Martha thought as she perused the desk for the ideal spot to place the carefully folded message written on aged parchment.

Martha knew exactly what to do. Christian had implored her to send a communication to his sister. He often watched over Addie and wanted her to feel his love and support. He also recognized that Clara would learn of the note—something that would benefit her as well.

Martha carefully placed Christian's note where only Addie could find it. With this mission complete, Saint Martha quickly departed, for a new novena was being said, and she needed to answer another loving soul's call.

Clara, Will, and Millie arrived at the Dorchester home late that evening. James was still visiting Addie and Teddy at the hospital, and the children were sleeping at their neighbor's home for the night. Clara unpacked in the guest room where they would stay for the next few weeks as Addie regained her strength and Teddy hopefully gained weight. Exhausted from their journey by ferry and train, they went to bed early to be refreshed in the morning.

The next morning, the children returned home, eager to see their grandparents and meet their little brother.

"Father, let's go to the hospital now to meet Teddy. I made a picture for him," Rose exclaimed to James. Warren, a delightful little toddler with Addie's wild, curly hair and big green eyes, kept chanting, "Teddy, Teddy," and then, "Brother," repeatedly.

"After breakfast, we will go to the hospital to see Teddy," James told his eager children. "Soon you will meet your new little brother and see your mother as well."

The children giggled with delight as Clara ushered them to the kitchen table for a hearty breakfast of eggs and bacon. Clara's breakfasts were truly legendary; her family had little understanding of how she had become so skilled with a skillet after many years serving breakfast and dinner to her guests at the inn in England.

Those days were merely a memory now, and Clara rarely allowed her thoughts to meander back to her youth in England, the loss of her parents, and then Arthur's death, followed by her leap of faith to marry Will and start anew on Prince Edward Island. Those memories were to be cherished but kept private; even Will never mentioned a word about that time.

"Best to leave it all alone; there's no reason to upset our beautiful family with my long-ago secrets," Clara said to herself, though she wasn't entirely sure she believed her own thoughts.

The family returned to Dorchester, and the house hummed with helpful grandparents, tired parents, busy youngsters, a dog, and a newborn.

Little Teddy had a voracious appetite and was gaining weight rapidly. His jaundiced complexion had transformed over the course of a few weeks to a warm glow. Addie was pleased but exhausted.

She often experienced overwhelming feelings of sadness and loss when remembering her brother Christian; at times, she still felt guilt for being such a precocious child and insisting on swimming that awful day. Now, baby Teddy, resting in her arms, was the spitting image of Christian; she wondered if her mother and father saw the resemblance as well.

James, Teddy, and Christian all melded into one person in Addie's tired, sleep-deprived mind.

Teddy was such a hungry baby that Addie had little time for anything other than his care. She felt terribly guilty about Rose and Warren but was always grateful that her capable parents were there to help. The children adored Clara and Will; however, they were very active and were exhausting their grandparents' energy.

Will was unable to make it through an entire day of watching the two youngsters without taking a substantial nap. This concerned Clara as she observed him continue to lose energy with each passing week that they stayed in Dorchester.

"Will, I don't like what I see regarding your health progress—or should I say regression—recently. I think you should discuss this with Doctor Pulin. The gains you made on Martha's Vineyard seem to be reversing with the hectic schedule we're keeping while helping with Rose and Warren," Clara stated definitively to her husband.

"Clara, what else can we do? Addie can't handle all of this right now with a baby who needs extra care and two active children. She would be devastated if we left to go back to the Vineyard."

"Will, I have an idea that may benefit several people. Remember the Walker family whom we often see on the Vineyard? Two of their four children are deaf, but they are fluent in sign language and get along beautifully on the island. The oldest daughter, Jane, is now twenty and eager to explore the world beyond the Vineyard; I briefly discussed the possibility of her coming here to Dorchester to assist Addie and James with the children, and she seemed very interested in the idea."

Will looked at Clara in surprise. "That is a lovely thought, my sweet Clara, but how can Jane be of assistance to Addie when she cannot communicate with the family?"

"I plan to teach them all—including Warren—how to sign." With that, Clara left their bedroom to discuss this exciting idea with Addie.

Addie felt depleted. She wished to see Teddy as her sweet new baby, but his need for near-constant feeding was overwhelming. He could go no longer than two hours without food, and when hungry, he would unleash an ear-piercing scream demanding it.

The doctor had indicated that Teddy could start on some solid food around ten or eleven months old. Now, at only two months of age, Addie had no idea how she would manage another nine months without sleep and this constant nursing. Whenever she had a free moment, Rose or Warren came running to her, vying to sit on her lap and wanting her to read to them, play games, and engage in the activities they all loved to do together before the baby arrived.

Clara would rush to place the sleeping baby in his bassinet, allowing Addie to enjoy a few moments with the children each afternoon. She also encouraged her daughter to spend a little time each day journaling or typing on the typewriter—anything to relieve her mind from the ongoing physical exhaustion.

"Addie, the children and I have a surprise for you this afternoon. When Teddy goes down for his nap, we will reveal something we have been working on together over the past few weeks."

Once Teddy was snug in his bassinet in his parents' room, Clara brought Addie to the living room. Today, Will was there too—forgoing his daily nap to see what the children had prepared for their mother.

The audience of three sat quietly in the living room as Rose and Warren bounded in joyfully.

"Mother, we have a surprise for you!" Rose said exuberantly. "And Warren is going to help me as much as he can. Ready, set, go!"

The two children stood side by side, beaming with huge smiles on their faces. No words emerged from their mouths. Instead, they utilized a variety of hand gestures that appeared to convey a message to the audience.

"Mother, did you enjoy our show?" Rose asked after four or five minutes of gesturing. She was quite expressive with her movements, which appeared to be some form of language that Warren would joyfully repeat.

Clara was beaming. "Children, that was wonderful! It's truly a beautiful message. Would you like to explain to your mother what you were doing?"

"Mother, don't you know we were signing a story? Grandmother has taught us Martha's Vineyard Sign Language, and now we can communicate with deaf people!"

Will put his arm around Clara; only she could have taught the little ones such a beautiful language in such a short time. The story she chose to teach them was characteristically Clara; it revolved around love and helping people discover how to communicate with one another.

Warren, still too young to fully understand the signing, could clench his fists and cross his arms over his chest like a bear hug—the sign for love.

Now it was time to inform Addie about their plan.

Addie was not entirely on board with the plan to have a deaf twenty-year-old woman—whom she had never met—come to live with her family. However, Clara insisted that this was the best arrangement for everyone involved. Addie could easily see that her father was not thriving in their home, and Clara was also exhausted. While someone younger might be a good idea, the communication barrier felt insurmountable.

But Clara was relentless and arranged daily signing lessons for Addie, James, and the other children. After two weeks, they were proficient enough, so Clara reached out to the Walkers to discuss the possibility of Jane coming for a visit to see if the arrangement might work.

That weekend, Clara and Will planned to meet Jane at the train station and bring her back to Dorchester. With four bedrooms in the house, they could all comfortably stay together for a week of training for Jane before Will and Clara returned to the Vineyard.

Jane waved from the train tracks as she spotted Clara and Will in the crowd at the station. She was a striking young woman with an athletic build and long copper hair. Her eyes were green with flecks of yellow that played in the sunlight, making them mesmerizing. She laughed easily and almost always wore a radiant smile. In many ways, she appeared otherworldly.

Jane had long known how to read lips, so it was easy for her to understand Will and Clara when they faced her while talking. She could also articulate many words, although her pronunciation was sometimes difficult to understand. But with a combination of lip reading, signing, and speaking, they managed to communicate just fine. Clara was certain that Jane would bring joy, resilience, and much-needed help and companionship to her daughter and the family.

It was time to bring Jane Walker home to meet the family.

It was Saturday, so the entire family was home. Teddy was taking a longer nap than usual, and James was in the yard with the children and Millie, playing catch. Addie could hear their laughter through the window. Realizing that she had a moment for herself, Addie decided to follow some of her mother's advice.

I haven't touched a typewriter in almost three months, she mused to herself. *Why don't I try journaling on the typewriter to practice the two skills I have neglected for so long?*

Addie sat at her secretary's desk and inserted a piece of paper into the typewriter. For some reason, it was jamming, and she couldn't get it in. Frustrated with herself and her lack of confidence in typing after this hiatus, she reached her hands inside the machine to see what was blocking the paper.

She felt around the keys—what was this? Her fingers brushed against a coarse paper of some sort, resembling an old parchment. She lifted it from where it was seemingly placed between the keys.

It appeared to be a note, written in cursive on the aged piece of paper. She unfolded it and gasped.

Addie,

    Never despair when you think of me, for I am happy here with my father and the angels. It's beautiful and full of light. I feel content and safe. I watch over you and know that you still have much to achieve. Please let Mother know that I am fine and that I love her. Also, let Will know I love him like a father.

    Your devoted brother, Christian

The memories of the day Addie found the mysterious vanishing note in her mother's desk flooded back to her.

The note was from a man named Arthur, who claimed to be Clara's husband.

First it was there, and then it was gone. Addie was mystified. Many secrets needed to be addressed in the Warren family, and she would have to speak to her parents immediately about them.

She looked down at the coarse parchment in her hands and reread the words once more. As she finished the last word, the paper disintegrated in her fingers, like grains of sacred sand, and simply disappeared.

CHAPTER 12

Reconciliation

We never truly know where our lives are headed; reality is fickle and resides in the eyes of the beholder. However, if you believe, you may find it easier to see the truth before you. Clara always understood this, and now Addie was learning it as well.

Addie had no time to absorb what she discovered in the typewriter. The note had vanished, possibly a figment of her imagination. Or was it genuinely a divine message from her deceased brother? She was exhausted from giving birth, constantly nursing, watching two young children, and attending to the needs of their household.

Perhaps she was daydreaming—maybe she had fallen asleep at her desk, and this was all just an illusion of her mind.

Had she found a note from her deceased brother, who had drowned years ago while trying to save her? It mentioned that he had a different father than hers. What kind of message was that? It truly seemed more fictional than real, and she should probably keep this to herself rather than confront her parents with such nonsense. Everyone would think that she was going mad from exhaustion.

Addie walked into the kitchen to get a glass of water; she could see her beautiful children playing with their father and Millie on the lawn in the backyard. The scene warmed her heart.

Addie loved James and the life they were living here in the States; she worshipped her parents and was so proud of all they had accomplished. While she dearly missed her siblings on Prince Edward Island, she knew she had found an equally wonderful place to call "home." Her parents had also found their own new nest on Martha's Vineyard—one that was calling them back. Addie understood that the Vineyard was a place where her parents were making a meaningful impact.

As Addie quietly observed her family, she first saw Rose—and then Warren—run to the side yard gate. There, she witnessed their joyful embrace with Clara, then Will, and finally a beautiful young woman who must be Jane Walker. Jane signed to both children, and they quickly engaged in their own form of chatter—each smiling and laughing as they conversed.

Interesting, Addie thought, that this woman could so easily communicate with her family. She continued to watch as James joined the conversation, signing to welcome Jane to their home. Clara and Will, fully immersed in the sign language exchange, appeared happier—and even healthier—than Addie had seen them in the past few months. A weight had been lifted from them, as they prepared to welcome this seemingly delightful young woman into the family.

Addie quickly checked on Teddy to ensure he was still asleep. He appeared full and content—a rarity! Addie walked out the back door to meet Jane and to gauge just how this arrangement might work out.

Jane saw Addie coming down the stairs into the backyard. Without hesitation, she walked over and signed, "Thank you for your kind offer to bring me to your home and meet your lovely family."

Addie was pleased that she understood the blend of speech and sign language, mentally nodding in appreciation to her mother for insisting that they all learn how to communicate in this manner.

A few minutes later, Teddy belted out one of his signature screeches, demanding immediate attention. Addie quickly made her way back to the house to retrieve him but noticed that Rose had grabbed Jane's elbow to alert her to the baby's cries.

Addie was proud of her daughter for understanding Jane's inability to hear Teddy and for informing her of the situation. Perhaps, as a family team, this arrangement might indeed work well.

Clara and Will stayed with Jane and the family to work out any hiccups in the new living situation. Rose and Warren shared one bedroom with twin beds, while Jane occupied another with a full bed. Addie and James had their own room, and Clara and Will used the guest room.

Addie planned to keep that room open for guests for now, but eventually, they would move the two brothers into one room once Teddy was older.

Clara was pleased with how well Jane blended into the family. She was a very capable young woman, and the children immediately took to her. They enjoyed playing games with Jane, walking through the neighborhood, and showing her the tree-lined streets of Dorchester.

Within just a few days, Jane was not only helping with childcare; she was also cooking Clara's favorite recipes to serve the family. Clara had taken great care to write them all down in a notebook—complete with ingredients and instructions on where to purchase any food items in town. Clara and Will took Jane on the streetcar into Boston, giving her a full tour of the city and ensuring she knew how to find the schedule and pay for each ride.

James couldn't be more relieved; Addie was already looking more relaxed. Clara was a miracle worker. Although everyone felt sad to see Clara and Will head back to Martha's Vineyard that Saturday, they all knew they were in good hands with Jane there.

Additionally, Addie and James both realized that her parents—now in their seventies—could not provide the daily assistance their family needed. It was simply too much for them, and Will's health was a primary concern.

It was decided that, in a few weeks, the Ryan family of five, including baby Teddy, would be accompanied by Jane for a visit to the Vineyard. There, they could meet Jane's family and finally see the island that had so captivated Clara and Will.

Clara, Will, and Millie were all relieved to be back on the island. Clara and Will missed the scent of the ocean, the endless expanse of the sky, the majestic waves, the red clay bluffs, and the miles of sandy beaches waiting to be explored. Millie, too, longed for her daily walks in the quaint town where everyone knew her name and loved to see her. Clara and Will also missed their roles in assisting the islanders with enticing tourism efforts, particularly focusing on "offseason" economic growth.

Martha's Vineyard offered a welcome respite for Clara and Will, serving as a place where they could thrive both physically and mentally.

"Clara, we need to find a place for Addie, James, and the children to stay when they come to the Vineyard next month. Unfortunately, they won't all fit in our little two-bedroom house for a three-night visit."

Clara made a few inquiries, and it was decided that the Harborview Hotel would be an excellent choice for the visit. They could reserve two adjoining rooms to create a small suite for the five Ryans. Jane would, of course, stay with her family, taking a few days off to catch up with her loved ones.

A few days before their scheduled train and ferry journey to the Vineyard, Jane made a request to Addie. Through her eloquent signing skills and Addie's willingness to learn this new language, the two communicated with ease.

"Miss Addie, may I meet you on Martha's Vineyard next weekend, perhaps a little later than your schedule? I have an appointment with the Horace Mann School for the Deaf in Boston next Friday morning about possibly becoming a teacher."

Addie felt both surprised and saddened. She believed that Jane enjoyed working for her family and was unaware that Boston had a school dedicated to the deaf. "Of course you may, Jane; I just assumed that you would be with our family for a few years, as you are such a wonderful and helpful presence."

Jane smiled and signed back, "While you are on the Vineyard this weekend, you will meet my younger sister, Emily, who is not deaf and is interested in taking college courses here in Boston. I think you will love her, and she will love you."

Addie was uncertain about the entire situation, but she had learned to be less controlling and to embrace the winds of change. "Well, I look forward to meeting Emily. If she is anything like you, I'm sure she will be wonderful."

The trip to Martha's Vineyard was very exciting for the Ryan family. Addie and James had never been there, and Rose and Warren were thrilled about taking a real train to New Bedford and then a ferry to the island. Teddy was beginning to sleep and eat more on a schedule, providing Addie with a welcome rest for a few hours each day and a longer night's sleep each night.

Jane had told Addie that although she wanted to visit her parents and siblings, she decided to stay in Dorchester for the entire weekend. She realized that if she were accepted as a teacher, she would need to find a suitable living arrangement for herself in Boston. The school had a placement program for its instructors, so it was best that she made constructive use of this time while the family was away; at least this is what she conveyed to Addie.

It was a long day of travel, but from the deck of the ferry, they could all see the outline of the Vineyard shoreline as they approached. They were surprised by the island's similarity to Prince Edward Island. There were red clay cliffs, white sandy beaches, homes built high on the bluffs, and waves glimmering in the sunlight. The sky appeared endless over the island's silhouette, with the fluffiest clouds they had ever seen frolicking above.

The ferry pulled into the dock in Cottage City, and the entire family was enchanted. A beautiful white wooden gazebo stood in the middle of the town common, visible from their perch on the ferry. It was surrounded by homes that resembled real-life gingerbread houses!

Clara had already informed the children about the Cottage City merry-go-round and promised to take them there on the weekend. For now, however, the family would be welcomed by a horse and buggy driver who would transport them to their grandparents' home in nearby Edgartown. The island had very few automobiles, so, in many ways, it felt like stepping back in time to be there.

"James, I honestly cannot believe my eyes. I cannot comprehend that this is part of the Commonwealth of

Massachusetts," Addie exclaimed as she held Teddy in her arms.

James was also intrigued by this island oasis. Since arriving in the Boston States, he had felt a sense of energy and purpose. Part of the city reminded him of his upbringing in Quebec City, which he had traded for the tranquility of Prince Edward Island to appease his parents. He had learned to love it there as well. Boston was a new adventure—something he could call his own, and he felt proud to be making his way there. James had created a new life for his family, and they were all thriving. Yet, this island just a few miles from the coast provided much of the peace and natural beauty that he so cherished on Prince Edward Island. They were now living in the best of both worlds—in a city that offered economic advancement and abundant stimulation, with an island getaway within reach.

"I can already see why your parents have fallen in love with this place. I cannot wait to explore it all with you and the children this weekend," James replied, kissing both Teddy and Addie on their foreheads and hugging Rose and Warren.

Addie had been so busy packing and keeping Teddy content during the day's trip that she had yet to find the right time to tell James of her surprising conversation with Jane.

"Oh, James, I received some sad news from Jane today. It turns out that in addition to visiting my parents, we will also be meeting Emily Walker, Jane's younger sister who has just completed her education on the island. Emily is interested in taking Jane's place with our family, as Jane has an interview today with a school for the deaf in Boston."

James was not as unprepared for this news as Addie had been; Jane was wonderful, but there was something else about her that made him feel she was destined to be with their family for only a short time. It was as if she had been sent to them for a reason, and that her mission might now be complete. Jane had perfectly fit into their family, teaching them all so much about individuals with disabilities and how they can flourish. He proudly reflected on how the children effortlessly learned to sign and how they adored Jane for her beautiful spirit. The difference in Addie since her arrival had been remarkable; and Addie had the time to write again, which was something of great importance to her.

"Well, I am sure this is all for a reason, and we look forward to meeting Emily this weekend while wishing Jane success with her interview," he responded calmly.

Back at the house on Chickatawbut Street, Jane quickly set to work. It wasn't common for Saint Martha to take on the form of an earth soul, but at times she believed it was the best way to assist those who needed her.

Disguised as Jane, Saint Martha could assist this young family in various ways. As Martha, she could stealthily share Christian's message with Addie. Moreover, Martha understood that this revelation—paired with Addie's discovery of Arthur's letter to Clara many years earlier—would be significant for the family and its future.

Martha mused, *There are times when secrets must be kept, and times when they must be shared and understood.* Martha was confident that the moment had come for Clara and Will to disclose this information to the family.

Becoming Jane was a wonderful way to integrate into the family and help Clara and Will return to the life they cherished on Martha's Vineyard. It was also an essential learning experience for the entire family, which would someday lay the foundation for Rose's future as an advocate for the disabled. Martha took comfort in knowing that the seeds she could sow would lead to future good.

But now, still in Jane's form, she had some work to do at the house. Soon, Addie would talk to Clara about the note she found from Christian. That conversation would trigger a series of revelations for the entire Warren family. Martha knew what she needed to do now . . . She sat down at the typewriter and inserted two pieces of paper with carbon between them, realizing she would have to do this multiple times to create enough of the precious notes for the entire family.

Saint Martha, in her human form as Jane, typed enough copies of the document for each of the Warren children. She remained optimistic that these messages would be passed down through generations in the family to offer a source of comfort and hope.

Seated at Addie's small secretary's desk, Jane placed her hands on the wood as she embraced her role as Saint Martha once more. This desk would now also provide comfort and guidance to its owners.

Saint Martha felt pleased. It was time to leave the house and head to Martha's Vineyard to help alleviate the challenges that lay ahead.

The buggy pulled up to the Harborview Hotel, which was just a short walk from Clara and Will's home. The five Ryans thanked the driver, whom Will had prepaid, and wished him well. The driver had been a wonderful source of island history, which they all enjoyed.

The hotel was grand and very exciting for everyone. Waiting on the large, covered porch were Clara, Will, and Millie. The joyous reunion was beautiful, Martha thought as she watched from a rocking chair in a far corner of the porch. *Let us hope this weekend goes well so that this family can finally learn and accept the truth*, she said to herself before vanishing into thin air.

Clara and Will had a full itinerary of island touring planned. But first, it was time to unpack from the day's journey. The hotel suite was on the second floor of the regal wood-clad hotel, featuring shiny floorboards and delicate wallpaper above the wainscoting, which reached halfway up the walls. Framed pictures on the walls illustrated the whaling history of Edgartown, and from their room, Addie and James and the children enjoyed a bird's-eye view of the town lighthouse. Clara had already arranged a morning tour with the hotel manager for the family to learn more about the hotel's history.

"And I will be honored to take care of Teddy while you are on the tour," Clara stated in a matter-of-fact manner when she informed the family of their morning itinerary.

"This evening, we will have dinner at our home at six o'clock; it is just a five-minute walk down North Water Street. I made sure to prepare all your favorite dishes," Clara mentioned as they unpacked their belongings in the elegant bureau drawers.

"Relax and settle in and we will see you in two hours," Clara said as she and Will headed out.

"Addie, your parents have more energy than we do. It seems they have a robust schedule for us this weekend. I hope we can keep up with them," James said with a laugh as he sat on the edge of the sumptuous bed.

"Yes, indeed they do," Addie replied. While she was proud of them both and all they had accomplished, Addie still ruminated about the mysterious message in the typewriter and the long-forgotten letter in her mother's desk. She decided it was time to share these findings with James, even if he believed she was imagining them.

Addie placed the baby in the crib that Clara had ordered for the room. With Rose and Warren in their adjoining room happily engaged in creative picture drawing, Addie sat down next to James on the bed.

"There are a few things I need to tell you, James, which I hope you will believe."

From there, she proceeded to tell the entire story, going into detail about Christian, their unique bond, the day he died, the note in her mother's desk from a possible earlier husband, and then the message from Christian found within the keys of the typewriter.

Addie's voice was nearly a whisper as she shared these revelations with James. After finishing, she gazed at his face to gauge his response.

"I believe all of it, Addie. I believe that Christian sent that message to you recently. Teddy's birth has strongly brought back his memory for you. Perhaps it is time to discuss with your mother the note you found in her desk. I am not sure what the explanation is, but it is time to put this tormenting secret you have held to rest."

Addie threw her arms around her husband. It felt as if a great burden had been lifted from her. It was time to learn the truth: Addie was not angry with her parents and knew they would never hurt her or her siblings. But it was time to learn more about their past so that they could all move forward.

Clara's preparation of the freshly caught bass was exceptional. She pan-roasted the fish with lemon and onion and served it piping hot on a bed of rice, accompanied by a garden salad with garlicky dressing. Clara also baked the children's favorite popovers, which were devoured within minutes as the delicious farmstand butter melted into them.

"Mother, you have outdone yourself with this meal," Addie complimented as she watched her children ask for second helpings.

Clara felt content: The meal was lovingly prepared, and she and Will were delighted that Addie and James had brought the family to the Vineyard. Now they would appreciate how this enchanted island had captured their hearts.

The conversation included learning about the full itinerary for the visit: the hotel tour, a day exploring Edgartown, an afternoon in Cottage City to see the gingerbread houses at the Methodist campground, ample time on the Carousel, shopping at the local farm, walks on the beach, and more. Clara had learned from Jane's family that Emily might become the family's new nanny, so she would be joining them for some of the activities as well.

"This all sounds wonderful, Mother, and we are grateful for the planning you have done for us. For now, though, do you mind if I have you to myself for a cup of tea and a little chat?"

Clara sensed the shift in Addie's voice. What did Addie want to discuss privately with her? "Yes, of course, dear. Instead of having a cup of tea together, why don't we take a walk toward the lighthouse and chat as we stroll?"

The summer evening was warm, with the sun just setting. "Yes, that sounds like a good plan," Addie agreed. Clara got Millie's leash, and the three said a quick goodbye to Will, James, and the children. "We will return shortly, loves. We just need a little private time together," Addie called to James and the children.

James nodded, understanding the situation perfectly.

Once out of earshot of the house, Addie started the difficult conversation.

She was neither combative nor defensive when explaining her experience of seeing the letter from Arthur in the desk. Addie was simply stating what she had been experiencing for a long time—that there was more to Christian's story.

Christian was always so different from the other siblings. While Bill, John, Louise, Emma, and Addie all had the "Warren look" with their round faces, green or blue eyes, and unmanageable curly brown hair, Christian was very pale, with light blue eyes and almost white hair. Yes, he resembled Clara, but there was also something unique about him.

Christian was so responsible, almost to a fault. He took on the weight of the world and had been Addie's greatest champion until the day he died.

Clara remained silent while Addie continued. She listened intently, absorbing every word Addie said.

As Addie spoke her truth, Clara embarked on a mental journey, her thoughts of England overwhelming her. In her mind, she pictured her parents, who passed away far too young. She envisioned her days working alongside Arthur, running the inn while he crafted timeless pieces of beauty in his woodwork shop.

She recalled the war and her first novena to Saint Martha, who had initially answered her prayers but then deeply disappointed her with Arthur's early death. Then, she remembered the terror of learning she was pregnant, without a husband.

But there was Will—always Will—by her side, providing love and unending support. Life had been hard, but it was also wonderful. How was it possible that things worked out? Was it Will, or was it Saint Martha, or was it just the road map of her life, and how she learned to navigate it?

"Addie, it is all true. I was married to a man named Arthur long ago in England. I was eighteen years old when I married him, and we owned an inn together. He was a war hero and a master woods craftsman, and I was a seamstress and the innkeeper. It was he who made my secretary's desk, which has always brought me comfort."

She softly continued, "And long ago, in the maple woods near where we lived, I saw a mysterious woman with long, flowing red hair and piercing green eyes who seemed to be a veritable angel, appearing to me near the tree Arthur had chosen to make the desk. Perhaps she was Saint Martha herself, as I had prayed the novena to save Arthur when he was at war. He did indeed return unharmed, but just a few years later, he fell ill and died the same time I found out I was pregnant with Christian."

Clara went on, "Your father was a friend to both Arthur and me. He often stayed at our inn. When Arthur died, your father offered me a path forward; he asked me to believe in him and to return to Prince Edward Island as his wife, raising the baby as his own.

"He did not demand my love, but he received it wholeheartedly over time. Your father possesses such dignity and grace, but most importantly, love and unending understanding. It was a mutual decision to keep Christian's lineage to ourselves."

Clara studied Addie's face for a clue as to how she was feeling. This was a difficult conversation, but one that needed to happen after all these years. Clara felt relief and anguish, as if they were one emotion. But it was time for the truth, first with Addie, and later with all their children.

Addie wrapped her arms around her mother. "Mother, you are so brave, and I don't fault you for what you and Father did. You have been wonderful parents, and you gave us what matters most—unconditional love. Christian's message to me was that he loved you so much and totally loved Will as his own father. He is happy where he is now with his other father, and he watches over all of us, as Saint Martha does."

The two had stopped walking and rested on the steps at the Harborview, watching the sky glow with the rays of sunset behind the lighthouse. Tears streamed down both their faces, and Millie snuggled between them, seeking to lick them away. Mother and daughter sat in a silence that was neither sad nor uncomfortable. Instead, it was a silence of deep understanding and gratitude that the truth was finally known. After a while, they got up to walk home and talk to Will and James; the children were too young to grasp what had just occurred, but the rest of Addie's siblings also needed to hear this important news.

Saint Martha had thoughtfully prepared a gift for each Warren sibling. She silently disappeared into the night, gliding from her hidden spot near Addie and Clara and then stealthily returning to the house where she would leave them all precisely what they needed.

Clara and Addie, with Millie in tow, returned about an hour after they had left. Both looked exhausted and as though they had been crying. Teddy was sound asleep in a crib that Clara had borrowed from a neighbor. The other two children had also nodded off on the couch.

James stood to greet his wife and mother-in-law. He recognized what had just occurred and felt proud of his wife for confronting such challenging events from the past with her mother.

Will, too, knew instinctively that a major discovery had been made, and together, the four talked through more of the past. A few hours later, the Ryans returned to their hotel room with their sleeping children in tow. There were no more secrets, and tomorrow, they would all enlighten the rest of the Warrens.

Emotionally exhausted, Clara sat at her desk to jot down a few notes before going to bed. Will had already retired to their room. She sat at Arthur's extraordinary desk, a constant in her life for decades, and felt the wood from which it was crafted. The wood from the enchanted maple where Saint Martha had once hidden. Clara's life journey had not been an easy one—it was filled with loss and disappointment, yet it also encompassed so much love and beauty. She felt grateful for the life she had lived and for Saint Martha.

Clara's prayers may not have been answered exactly as she wished, but Saint Martha had given her the strength and resilience to move forward. The novena had been a part of her life since childhood, yet in this moment, Clara understood its power more profoundly. The novena introduced Martha into Clara's life, but it was Clara who had to navigate through life. Saint Martha was always there as a guide, a supporter, and a loving presence.

Clara paused to contemplate what awaited her the following day. Informing the rest of the family would be challenging, but she and Will could manage it. Their love would see them through.

Clara thought, *If only I could give each of them a copy of the novena. It would greatly enhance their understanding of my journey.* As she glanced down at her desk, she was astonished to see five neatly typed copies of the novena perfectly stacked atop five envelopes—one for each of their living children.

She read the words carefully, all typed in capital letters, from the novena that she had first recited at eighteen years old.

NOVENA TO ST. MARTHA

ST. MARTHA, I RESORT TO YOUR PROTECTION
AND FAITH. I OFFER THIS CANDLE WHICH I
SHALL BURN EVERY TUESDAY. COMFORT ME IN
MY DIFFICULTIES, AND THROUGH THE LODGING
OF THE SAVIOR IN YOUR HOUSE, INTERCEDE
FOR ME AND MY FAMILY THAT WE MAY HOLD
GOD CLOSE IN OUR HEARTS AND BE PROVIDED

FOR IN ALL NECESSITIES. I BESEECH THEE, ST. MARTHA, THAT I MAY BE ABLE TO OVERCOME ALL DIFFICULTIES AS THOU DIDST THE DRAGON WHICH WAS AT YOUR FEET.

OUR FATHER, HAIL MARY, GLORIA THREE TIMES

THIS PRAYER IS TO BE RECITED EACH TUESDAY, A CANDLE LIGHTED, AND A COPY OF THE PRAYER TO BE LEFT IN THE CHRUCH TO HELP SOME OTHER SOUL IN DISTRESS AND SUPPORT DEVOTION TO ST. MARTHA. THIS MIRACULOUS SAINT GRANTS EVERYTHING, NO MATTER HOW DIFFICULT, BEFORE THE EIGHTH TUESDAY.

Saint Martha's mission for Clara was now complete. It had been an honor for her to assist Clara and then Addie, and she hoped that each of the Warrens would cherish the gift of this novena and pass it down to their families—and to others—to provide comfort when needed.

EPILOGUE

Rose sat at her desk, reflecting on the developments of the past year. She took out her journal to record her thoughts on the numerous changes it had brought.

Her beloved grandparents Clara and Will Warren were in their late eighties and living independently on Martha's Vineyard. Much to the chagrin of her mother, Addie; her father, James; and all her aunts and uncles on Prince Edward Island, her grandparents purchased a historic home on the Vineyard fifteen years ago and settled there year-round. Instead of living in Boston with her parents or returning to their original home on Prince Edward Island, the two declared the Vineyard their "last stop" and chose to stay for the long run.

All was fine until, of course, it wasn't. Her grandfather Will, a strong man who battled heart failure for decades, finally succumbed to the disease in April. One evening, he kissed his wife of over seventy years good night and went to bed; Clara snuggled in later that evening, never noticing how still her dear husband had become.

But the morning brought the heartbreaking revelation that he had passed. "Will, please wake up," Clara cried, knowing in her heart what had transpired during the night. After holding him in her arms for what felt like hours, Clara forced herself to call the local hospital and her family.

Rose reflected on her grandmother Clara and her extraordinary marriage to her grandfather. If there were ever two "soulmates," it was them. The entire family was devastated. Grandpa Will made every one of his children and grandchildren feel special. He never missed a birthday and always kept in touch. It was as if the heart of the family had been torn out.

Grammy Clara was deep in grief but insisted on staying in their home on the Vineyard after the family returned from Will's funeral, which was held back on Prince Edward Island. It was a magnificent memorial held at the church that the Warrens had attended for generations. The day was a beautiful send-off for a caring and accomplished husband, father, grandfather, sibling, uncle, friend, and community member. Many residents remarked on how Will and his family had made such an impact for those on Prince Edward Island.

Rose's mother, Addie, was frantic because her mother, Clara, was planning to live alone back on the Vineyard, far from family, upon their return to the States. However, Clara was a headstrong woman who had endured much loss; she insisted she would be fine.

That August, Rose and her brothers, Warren and Teddy, each spent time with their grandmother on the island. Rose was now twenty-one, Warren was nineteen, and Teddy, sixteen. All still lived at home in Dorchester with their parents, so a week's visit to the charming Martha's Vineyard was a welcome adventure.

It was a different type of visit to the Vineyard this year, though. Clara went to great lengths to maximize the time she had with her grandchildren, sharing stories of past challenges, resilience, and hope.

"Let me tell you about England and the inn," she would begin, finally able to give them a glimpse of her origins. She would share the entire story with each of them—something they had heard whispered about while growing up but would now fully understand.

Clara discussed her first marriage, their uncle Christian, and her enduring love for Will. Finally, she shared with each of them about Saint Martha and the novena, including the importance of her secretary's desk, crafted by her first husband, Arthur, many years ago.

The three grandchildren learned more that summer than they had in all their years of schooling. Each felt an incredible bond with their mysterious and magical grandmother as they watched her mourn the love of her life while continuing with her own.

Upon returning to Dorchester, Teddy and Warren resumed school, while Rose returned to work. Rose had chosen an unexpected profession that had been nurtured since her childhood. Rose always remembered that when she was five years old, her grandmother brought the family a wonderful nanny named Jane Walker from Martha's Vineyard. Rose fondly recalled Jane, who had a significant impact on her life. Jane was deaf, and Clara taught Rose and Warren sign language so they could communicate with her.

Rose cherished this skill. She was fortunate to have two parents who insisted that all their children receive a higher education, and she had recently completed her studies at the all-women's Wellesley College in Massachusetts. There, she studied English with the aim of becoming a writer like her mother, which thrilled Addie, who still wrote features for the *Boston Globe*.

But Rose remained interested in helping the hearing impaired. After graduation, she visited the Horace Mann School for the Deaf and Hard of Hearing in Boston, where she had been told Jane Walker had taught many years ago. She often thought of Jane, her enchanting personality, and stunning natural beauty; Rose frequently mused that Jane was an "earth angel."

Rose went to the school to inquire about employment. Due to her exceptional signing ability, she was hired as a hearing teacher for the deaf. She loved the school, the students, and the faculty. Rose felt truly alive there, and Addie and James were both very proud of their daughter's decision, which was indeed a vocation.

While at the school, Rose tried to find records of Jane Walker. Nothing indicated that she had worked there, and no one recalled meeting her. Rose shrugged it off but frequently thought of Jane while on campus.

"Mother, what do you recall about Jane Walker? I can't find any trace of her at the school," Rose asked Addie one afternoon.

"All I know, dear Rose, is that she was enchanting, almost like an angel walking among us," Addie replied. "She was here one moment and gone the next. Yet her brief stay with our family ignited your passion. Perhaps that was one of her missions in this life."

The fall was a busy time, and James and Addie were still actively involved in their respective professions, although Addie was spending more time engaging with the Boston social scene. As patrons of the Isabella Stewart Gardner Museum, Addie and James frequently attended performances there. It was a lovely period in their lives, with their three children happily pursuing their own endeavors.

As they became immersed in their respective worlds, their worry for Clara, who was alone on the Vineyard, lessened. Weekly phone calls from Addie, James, and the grandchildren delighted Clara as she listened to each one describe their studies and multifaceted work. Clara also tried to stay busy by volunteering at a local food pantry on the island and scheduling dinners with her many friends there.

Yet each day was a struggle for Clara, who missed Will to her core. Sometimes, she felt his presence in the living room, sitting by the fire in his favorite armchair. She talked to the chair as if Will were right there with her, and she believed she felt his comforting embrace while she slept. Yet, she kept her sad thoughts to herself each week when conversing with her children and grandchildren.

Often, she would speak aloud to the love of her life. "Will, I'm not sure how much longer I can stay here without you," Clara addressed her imagined husband in the chair. "My spirit is with you, and I hope to join you soon."

As Christmas drew near that year, Addie and James urged Clara to visit them for a few weeks. Was it the loneliness that led Clara to agree? No one knew what made her acquiesce, but soon, arrangements were made for Clara to travel back to Dorchester for the holidays.

When she arrived, Clara looked thin and weary. She was frail and used a cane to support her balance while walking. Everyone was shocked at her decline.

The guest room was prepared for her, and Clara went to bed early that first night. Addie knew her mother would soon want to join her father; life without Will seemed unbearable.

The next morning, Addie and Rose formulated a plan: They would try to engage Clara during the holidays by trimming the tree and preparing a special dinner featuring one of her favorite recipes. They would do whatever they could to make this first Christmas without Will a little bit merrier.

James went to the local fishmonger and returned with fresh cod; tonight, the ladies would bake it with lemon juice and a topping of breadcrumbs and butter. Oven-roasted potatoes with Clara's favorite horseradish and sour cream, along with sautéed green beans, would accompany the meal. Clara's famous popovers with whipped butter would be the first course served.

It was a lovely evening. The family took turns adding ornaments to the tree, and everyone enjoyed the dinner. Clara was unusually quiet throughout the evening but drank in the love that was all around her.

"Grammy, may we ask you a few questions about Jane Walker?" Rose inquired while Clara dozed by the fire.

The question instantly brought Clara back to the present. "What do you want to know about her, Rose?"

"Well, I remember her fondly; she inspired me to become a teacher for the deaf. I will never forget how you taught us sign language before we met Jane. Communicating with her was easy—it was almost as if she could read my mind."

Clara smiled. Indeed, Jane was a wonderful addition to the family during her short stay. She reminded Clara of her brief encounter with Saint Martha decades ago. Clara pondered that thought deeply—or was it a revelation?

"Rose, perhaps you should search a bit more diligently for Jane. She could be an exceptional mentor to you. Spend some extra time seeking her out," Clara finally replied.

And with that, Clara excused herself to her room to embrace a peaceful sleep. It would be the last time the family saw her.

The next day, Clara did not wake at her usual 6:00 a.m. Addie finally entered her room a little after seven to check on her. There, she found her mother with her journal on her lap. She must have fallen asleep while writing, but she never woke up. Addie knew immediately what had transpired.

Her journal lay wide open for all to see; the entry read:

Dear Will, I miss you so . . . I am now ready to come to you. Please gather Christian, Arthur, and my parents to greet me. Also, if you see Saint Martha, let her know that I appreciate all that she has done for us.

When James entered, Addie was crying with her mother in her arms. Rose and her brothers soon followed. They bid farewell to their grandmother as Saint Martha observed, with Clara by her side.

Clara was buried beside her beloved Will in the Warren family plot in Charlottetown, Prince Edward Island. The service was just as lovely as Will's, just a few months earlier. Clara's impact on the island community was significant due to her generous spirit and the ongoing success of Christian's Caring House, as well as her former work in tourism. The church and post-service reception were filled with the many people who cherished Clara and Will Warren.

Addie and James were happy to spend over a week with Addie's siblings on the island, which also allowed many cousins to enjoy time together. It was a heartfelt tribute to a remarkable woman who had touched so many lives.

Soon after returning to Dorchester, Addie and James began making plans for the Vineyard house. The home was small but located in a lovely area of downtown Edgartown, featuring a long backyard that sloped down toward the water. Clara and Will had set up benches at the end of the lawn to watch the boats meandering in and out of the harbor.

"Addie, perhaps we should keep the house as a vacation spot for our family and for your brothers and sisters who may want to visit," James contemplated.

"I would hate to see it sit empty during the offseason," Addie replied. "It is such a sweet home, and my mother's desk is there. At some point, we should bring it back here to Boston."

However, Saint Martha had different plans for the Vineyard home—and for Arthur's desk.

Rose took her grandmother's words about finding Jane Walker to heart. Jane might have some of the answers she was seeking. However, she felt confused about her grandmother's comments regarding the significance of the desk, as well as Clara's long-ago encounter with a possible saint.

Rose wondered: Was Clara succumbing to dementia after Will's death, or was there more to the tales? *Honestly*, Rose thought to herself, *this family has far too many secrets!*

She was determined that Jane Walker would no longer remain a secret and that she would find her. Rose continued to ask about her at the school.

Saint Martha sensed Rose's thoughts and concluded that a chance encounter with Jane Walker at the Horace Mann School would serve as an excellent opportunity to assist her.

The following day, after her last class, Rose was called into the principal's office. She bounded over to the executive offices, eager to meet the principal, whom she greatly admired, thinking that perhaps there was a new assignment for her.

As she entered the office, a beautiful, middle-aged woman with auburn hair pulled back in a bun and dazzling green eyes turned around. Her skin glowed, and there were only a few streaks of white in her well-coiffed hair.

The woman smiled and signed, "Hello, Rose. It is wonderful to see you after all these years. I hear you are a truly remarkable teacher here at the school."

Rose could hardly believe her eyes. It was Jane Walker, standing right in front of her!

Jane had come to the school with a mission. There was an urgent need for a sign language teacher on Martha's Vineyard, and she wondered if Rose knew anyone who might be interested in the role.

They quickly engaged in lively banter. The principal then left for a meeting, permitting them to reconnect in his office.

Rose sat upright at the desk. The beautiful, magnificent desk. She mused to herself as she felt the smooth, warm maple under her hands. *How could this special heirloom desk provide so much comfort and guidance?*

Rose was happy and content. She was working on the island in a fulfilling capacity, making many new friends and often receiving visits from her family. She had also begun meeting a handsome young man for coffee regularly—who happened to be deaf—not that it was any issue for Rose, as she was fluent in sign language.

Life was moving in the right direction, all thanks to a chance meeting with Jane Walker just a few months ago.

"What remarkable luck!" Rose had exclaimed to her parents. "I landed my dream job on Martha's Vineyard—and to top it off, I can stay at my grandparents' beautiful home!" Even Addie understood there was more to this than incredible luck. Gazing upward, she thanked her mother, Clara, and Saint Martha.

For now, Rose was the newest and most appreciative resident of the Vineyard home, proudly claiming her place at the desk. Little did she know that her greatest adventures were yet to unfold.